FREEDOM TRAP

Books by Robert Elmer

AstroKids

Promise of Zion

Adventures Down Under

The Young Underground

PROMISE *of* ZION 5

FREEDOM
TRAP

ROBERT ELMER

BETHANY HOUSE PUBLISHERS
MINNEAPOLIS, MINNESOTA 55438

Published by Bethany House Publishers
A Ministry of Bethany Fellowship International
11400 Hampshire Avenue South
Bloomington, Minnesota 55438
www.bethanyhouse.com

Printed in the United States of America by
Bethany Press International, Bloomington, Minnesota 55438

Library of Congress Cataloging-in-Publication Data

Elmer, Robert.
    Freedom trap / by Robert Elmer.
        p.   cm. — (Promise of zion ; 5)
Summary: On the eve of Israel's independence in 1948, Emily is on her way back to England when she is delayed on Cyprus, where she finds the mother of her friend Dov, a Jewish refugee from Poland, and Emily is determined to let Dov, back in war-torn Jerusalem, know that his mother is alive.
    ISBN 0-7642-2313-5 (pbk.)
    1. Palestine—History—1917–1948—Juvenile fiction. [1. Palestine—History—1917–1948—Fiction.] I. Title.
    PZ7.E4794 Fr   2002
[Fic]—dc21   2001005682

To my father, Knud Elmer—

Like a tree planted by streams
of water, which yields its
fruit in season and whose leaf
does not wither.

—Psalm 1:3

ROBERT ELMER is the author of several other series for young readers, including ADVENTURES DOWN UNDER and THE YOUNG UNDERGROUND. He got his writing start as a newspaper reporter but has written everything from magazine columns to radio and TV commercials. Now he writes full time from his home in rural northwest Washington state, where he lives with his wife, Ronda, and their three busy teenagers.

CONTENTS

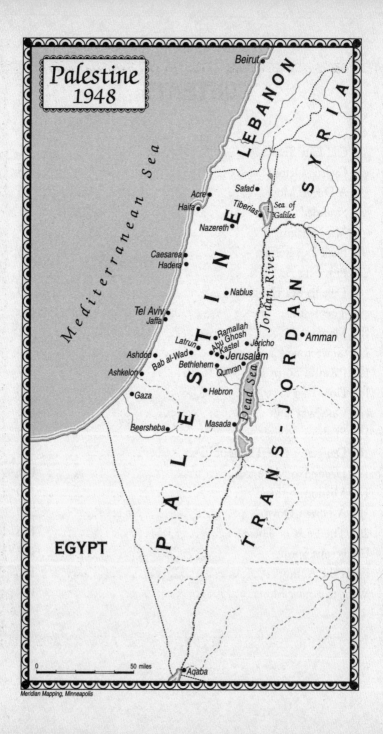

Palestine
1948

Beirut

LEBANON

SYRIA

Mediterranean Sea

Acre
Haifa
Safad
Tiberias
Sea of
Galilee
Nazereth

P
A
L
E
S
T
I
N
E

Caesarea
Hadera

Nablus

Jordan River

Tel Aviv
Jaffa

Ramallah
Abu Ghosh
Latrun
Castel
Jericho
Amman

Ashdod
Bab al-Wad
Jerusalem
Bethlehem
Qumran

Ashkelon

Dead Sea

Hebron

T
R
A
N
S
-
J
O
R
D
A
N

Gaza

Beersheba
Masada

EGYPT

0   50 miles

Aqaba

Meridian Mapping, Minneapolis

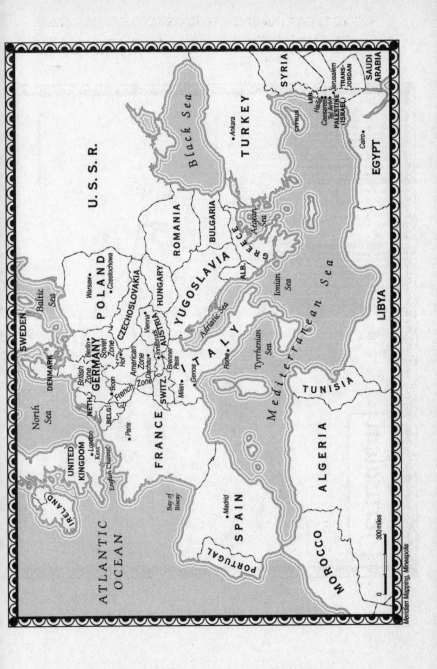

Meridian Mapping, Minneapolis

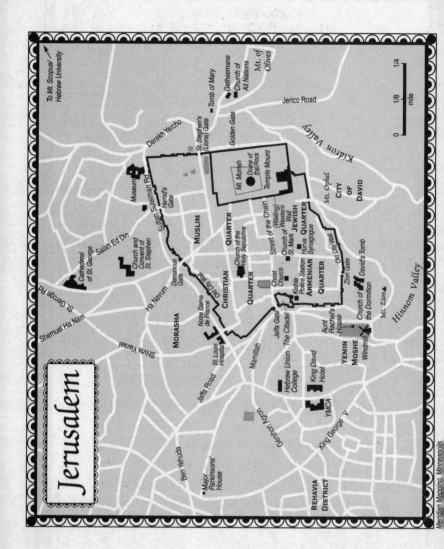

Jerusalem

To Mt. Scopus/
Hebrew University

Tomb of Mary
Gethsemane
Church of
All Nations
Mt. of
Olives

Jerico Road

Derekh Yercho

St. Stephen's
(Lions) Gate
Golden Gate

Museum
Sultan Suleiman Rd.
Herod's Gate

Mt. Moriah
Dome
of the Rock
Temple Mount

Kidron Valley

Salah Ed Din

Cathedral
of St. George

St. George Rd.

Church and
Convent of
St. Stephen

MUSLIM

QUARTER

Street of the Chain
Church of Western
the Holy Sepulchre (Wailing) Wall

Mt. Ophel

CITY
OF
DAVID

Church of the
Holy Sepulchre

JEWISH QUARTER

Ha Nevum

Damascus
Gate

CHRISTIAN

QUARTER

St. Mark's
Hurva
Synagogue

Shemuel Ha Navi

Old City Wall

Notre Dame
de France

Christ
Church

Police Station
Kishle

ARMENIAN
QUARTER

Old City Wall

Zion Gate

David's Tomb

Shivte Yisrael

MORASHA

Old City Wall

Jaffa Gate

The Citadel

Church of
the Dormition

Mt. Zion

Hinnom Valley

St. Louis
Hospital

Mamillah

Aunt
Rachel's
House

YEMIN
MOSHE

Windmill

Jaffa Road

Hebrew Union
College

King David
Hotel

Ben Yehuda

Gershon Agron

YMCA

King George V

REHAVIA
DISTRICT

Major
Parkinson's
House

0   1/8   1/4
mile

Meridian Mapping, Minneapolis

OLD CITY TRAP

Jerusalem
April 19, 1948

"Down!" Reb Herschel shouted a warning as the windowpane shattered into a million pieces on the living room floor.

Thirteen-year-old Dov Zalinski didn't need to be told. He tumbled to the floor behind the man's old, comfortable easy chair and put his arms around the two little girls with him. Golda and Haviva sobbed in fear. They probably wanted to be near their uncle, their mother . . . anyone but Dov, a stranger in their home.

"Shh. It's all right," Dov whispered, though he didn't believe a word of it. What could possibly be all right about this? The window now gaped like a broken-toothed grin punched out by a bully from the other side of Jerusalem's Old City walls.

What could be all right about this? he asked himself once more as they huddled behind the flowered chair. Haviva held her hands over her ears, but they wouldn't stop the next burst of gunfire.

"Golda? Haviva?" their mother called from the other side of the room. From the sound of things, Dov guessed Mrs. Elazar was pinned under the window with her brother-in-law, Herschel, and her youngest daughter, four-year-old Naomi. He couldn't tell which side of the room was in more danger just then.

"We're over here," Dov loudly whispered back between more thunder bursts of shellfire. "We're okay."

Not quite. In fact, they were most certainly *not* okay, kneeling in the remains of the living room window. From the Elazar living room, Dov could look out through the empty window up at the Old City wall and imagine the rest of Jerusalem beyond that. They were so close, in this crooked house on the Street of the Steps, to the shadow of the ancient outside wall.

That, of course, was the reason for the danger they now found themselves in. What else had Dov expected when he'd crawled through Mr. Bin-Jazzi's tunnel with his brother, Natan, just two days ago? If he'd hoped to tell the story to the world, the story of how Jewish Old Jerusalem was fighting for her life, he'd certainly come to the right place.

As long as they don't shoot up my transmitter. So much for the Voice of the *Haganah*, Israel's main army of volunteer freedom fighters. Dov peeked around the chair to where he had stowed his small shortwave radio device.

Five-year-old Haviva's fearful sobbing grew louder.

"It'll be over in a minute," Dov whispered. "Here, you want my apple?"

But Haviva just kept her forehead to the floor and shook like a leaf. So Dov stuffed the crab apple back into his pocket. It was mostly bruised, anyway.

A year older than Haviva, Golda kept one arm around her younger sister and the other around Dov. He'd already noticed Golda was the leader in neighborhood games up and down the stairs or out in the *Batei Machse* Square, where the kids played Kick the Can. She was the one who seemed to yell "One, two, three red herring!" the loudest, too.

I don't think they're going to be playing too many more games out there now. Dov clenched his teeth. *Not after this attack.*

If he had wanted to, Dov guessed he could toss a well-aimed stone over the nearby Old City wall through the hole where the window had once been. The small, warm house where Dov had found a place to stay guarded a spot in the wall's shadow halfway between the Zion and Dung Gates. Their attacker could be hiding anywhere over in the Arab neighborhoods clustered around Mount Ophel. Beyond that lay the Kidron Valley, then part of Jerusalem called the Silwan.

The idea of trading stones for bullets was silly, of course. A joke. But this attack surely wasn't.

"Is this the war Uncle Herschel has been telling us about?" asked Haviva.

Uncle Herschel. Not Dov's uncle, of course, but the girls'. Dov called him *Reb* Herschel—like Mr. Herschel, a name of respect.

Dov had been afraid to ask what had become of the girls' father. Away? Killed? In any case, Dov was surprised Haviva had found her tongue so quickly.

He shook his head. "The war hasn't begun yet. Two more weeks. Then comes the real war."

With bullets breaking their window, it seemed odd to say, but he knew what his older brother had told him was true. Reb Herschel had said the same thing. Two more weeks and the British would leave Palestine. Two more weeks and the Jewish people would declare their independence after nearly two thousand years. Two more weeks and they could begin to live in peace, in their own country. There was only one problem. . . .

Crack!

Another Arab bullet found its mark through the gaping wound in the window. This one buried itself with a sickening crackle in the wood trim on the far side of the Elazar living room—perhaps two feet from Dov's nose. Haviva shrieked. And Dov decided the overstuffed chair wasn't much of a shield, after all.

"Reb Herschel." Dov raised up on his knees. "I've got Golda and Haviva."

"Down the stairs, then," decided the man. "We'll be right behind you."

Dov flinched at the sound of another boom, like distant thunder, and then a crash. But this time the shooter must have shifted his target. They heard a thud from somewhere outside and then the dull tinkle of crumbling rock. Perhaps this round had hit the side of the house.

Now was the time to move.

"Come on, girls." Dov tried to pull them up by the shoulders. It wasn't as hard as he'd feared; Golda and Haviva weren't about to let Dov leave them. "We've got to get out of here."

The question was, to where? He froze at the top of the stairs, his knees suddenly turning to noodles.

Ta-ta-ta-ta-ta. A fresh round of gunfire filled the young night with bone-chilling echoes.

"Wh-what's *that*?" dark-eyed little Naomi wondered aloud.

"Machine gun," answered Reb Herschel. He took her in his arms. "But don't worry about a thing. It's still far away."

Dov shivered at the cold breeze that filled the living room. Naomi grabbed her uncle's gray beard as reins and rode his shoulders down the stairs.

The other girls gripped Dov's hands as if their lives depended on it. And maybe they did. Dov sighed with relief at the darkness outside the front door. At least now they would not be a target anyone could see.

"Which way?" Mrs. Elazar asked.

As if in answer, a flashlight snapped on and lit up their faces. Dov blinked in surprise until he heard his brother's voice.

"Is everyone all right here?" It didn't matter that Natan Israeli was only nineteen, just five and a half years older than Dov. He looked tough as a pirate, thanks to the shock of black hair poking out of the bandage across his forehead. And in the stark shadows behind the flashlight, he held his shoulders proudly and stiffly, as if he was every bit in charge.

Naturally. Wasn't he a member of the *Irgun*? The small, radical Jewish group prided itself on being tough and fearless, on doing *whatever it took* to win Jewish freedom. Their ways and ideas were rough, dangerous, frightening at times. Even so, Natan had wanted to sneak in with Dov to join the ragtag group of Haganah defenders, now trapped in the Jewish Old City. He'd insisted, even. That had to count for something.

"We're all right." Reb Herschel looked around as if to double-check that they were. One, two . . . all three of the girls.

Dov was still holding Golda's and Haviva's clammy hands when his brother's light found them once more. "They were scared, Natan."

Dov didn't have to explain himself. Natan waved for them to follow, then switched off his light—just as another burst of gunfire whined off the stone wall behind them.

"Oh!" Mrs. Elazar stumbled over Dov's heels, and he tried to help her up from the slick cobblestone, still wet from the late-afternoon rain.

"Hurry!" Reb Herschel grabbed his sister-in-law by the waist and dragged her on. Dov and the girls quickly followed. Only, where were they going?

"Come on, come on!" Up ahead, a hunched man waved a flickering kerosene lantern at them. They hurried around the corner, putting one more layer of buildings between them and the crazy shooting. And then the man was at the door of a ground-floor apartment, still waving his lantern.

"Herschel!" Mrs. Elazar gasped and pulled back for a moment. "Not the Liebermans'."

Reb Herschel didn't answer; a thunderous explosion of shells behind them spoke for him. It was the Liebermans' or the street.

"Of course there's room for six more." Mrs. Lieberman looked just as old as her husband, stooped and wrinkled. She waved them in as if they were stray cats.

"But we can't impose on you like this." Mrs. Elazar still didn't sound sure.

Impose! Dov was in no mood for a street camp-out.

"Nonsense." Mrs. Lieberman smiled. "You stay here as long as you need to."

But when Dov stepped inside he saw why Mrs. Elazar had held back. She must have known how small the Lieberman apartment was. Compared to the roomy two-story flat they'd just escaped, well, this was a closet. A small sitting room was barely large enough for a few people to sit in, knee-to-knee, on the floor—when it wasn't doubling as a bedroom or a dining room. At least there was a tiny, separate kitchen with a closet. The two women were given the honor of sitting in the apartment's only two chairs, while the three girls piled onto one of the narrow beds.

"Here," said Mr. Lieberman, sounding like a host at a dinner party. "We'll push this table over against the wall. Plenty of room."

Plenty of room. Dov stood by the door, wondering what had happened to his brother. But Natan had faded back into the night, the way he always seemed to.

"Some tea, Savta. Please." Mr. Lieberman pointed in the direction of the kitchen. "We should fix our guests some hot tea."

His wife shot him a look, a quiet message of some kind. He blinked and nodded. Message received.

"Well, as you know, most of us are a bit short on kerosene. Perhaps someone will get through the barricades tomorrow with more. But until then, please make yourselves comfortable with a cup of nice, cold water."

Dov almost smiled at the sound of the words. *"Make yourselves comfortable."* Another volley of shots sounded outside, and he peeked out the front door, just to make sure Natan wasn't out there somewhere. Like Dov, he, too, had made it to the Promised Land after the nightmare in Europe had separated their family. And now, here was Natan, helping to defend the remaining Jews in the walled-in Old City.

Tough-guy Natan.

"Did you see that?" Golda had joined him at the door. She pointed out into the darkness at a shadow that . . . "There! It moved!"

"I saw it, too," Dov whispered. He could not take his eyes off the shadows. An invader? A soldier? He gripped the edge of the door, ready to slam it shut.

CYPRUS DETOUR

Emily Parkinson squinted at the scribbled name on the napkin in her hand.

"Mr. Nick . . ." she read out loud, "Papa-*coast*-us."

She sighed and looked around her at the narrow alleyway. The dead end piled with crates of rotting purple eggplant told her she might be close to the right place. But where was this Mr. Nick Papakostas, seller of the finest vegetables on beautiful Cyprus Island? His cousin Spiro the dock worker had promised Emily she could ride along on one of his cousin's delivery runs to the detention camps.

"Yes, yes, of course," Spiro had told her.

For a fee, I'm sure. Emily wondered how much.

"I am sure Cousin Nick will be delighted," Spiro had said, just before launching into stories about his twenty-two other cousins.

Was everyone on this island related? The connections seemed almost as tangled as the ancient cobbled streets of Famagusta.

"Past the Old Sea Gate . . ." She tried to recall the directions the dock worker had given her when her ship had been towed in for repairs the night before. That was after they had picked up the boatload of Jewish refugees. Upon docking, though, the refugees had been whisked off the ship before anyone knew what had happened. "Security precautions," she'd been told.

"Two blocks, then right. Past the Cathedral of Saint Nicolas, then right again. No—left. Where *are* you, Mr. Papakostas?"

A low, throaty growl from behind a pile of castoffs was not the answer she wanted to hear—especially not when it was joined by another, and a third. She looked for a way to escape, but she could only return the way she'd come, and that would take her right back past the sound—inches from the growling.

Oh dear. Emily backed into a dark corner, hoping to blend into the old stone wall. *Perhaps I shouldn't have wandered away from the group.*

But how else would she find Nick Papakostas? And without him, how else would she get into the British detention camps to search for Dov's mother?

If she's ever even been here.

Emily had only the faintest hope of finding Mrs. Zalinski. Even so, now that Emily was delayed on Cyprus, she had to try. She'd promised Dov she would help him in his search. Now that promise was the only bridge remaining that linked Emily to the home where she had grown up. Jerusalem. Her *real* home. Not England.

For the past couple of days she'd been traveling on a ship sailing west, soon to be "back" in England, as her parents said. Back on the old estate in Kent, the one she could barely remember. There, she would be safely away from the gathering storm clouds of war that hung over Palestine. This strange island of Cyprus was only a short stopover on a trip that took her farther and farther from her heart—and her promises.

But what now? Did anyone know Emily was cornered by a pack of rather grumpy alley dogs on Cyprus? The mottled gray-

and-black leader showed his teeth in greeting, and the hair on the back of his mangy neck stood up as straight as that on Emily's. Emily considered screaming.

"Nice doggie." She held out her hand, which only brought the other two dogs out even more. Now she faced three sets of razor-sharp teeth. "My father's a very important officer in the British army, you know. And you really mustn't—"

This isn't working. Quickly, she raised her voice and stamped her foot. "Shoo!"

The leader of the pack snapped and advanced with a wild, fiery glint in his eye. This was no nice doggie.

"Yaah!" Emily shouted as loudly as she could this time and clapped her hands. She picked up a shattered crate as a shield, but she feared it would not be enough against the trio. The ribs showing through their sides proved they were hungry enough to . . . to what?

Please help me, Lord, Emily prayed silently, even as she desperately searched the wall behind her for one last chance at escape. And there it was! A heavy wooden doorway almost blended into the corner, and she inched her way toward it, her back to the cold stone.

"Take it easy," she whispered, and it occurred to her it would have been nice to have her Great Dane along on this walk.

Or maybe not. Big as he was, old Julian would have been no match for these mongrels.

There! She grabbed the old door handle and twisted just as the dogs lunged. But instead of turning, the handle came off in her hand. And in the last second of grace she owned, Emily reacted by throwing the brass door knob straight at the lead dog's nose.

Yip! The dog widened its eyes for a moment, long enough to take a breath before attacking.

Emily pounded on the door behind her with both fists. "Open

up!" she cried at the top of her lungs. "Help!"

But the door remained closed as yet another wild screaming and howling rushed down the alley at them.

More dogs? If it was, these three didn't know it. The shrieking typhoon washed down the alley, a tide of howls and windmilling arms.

"Out of here, you mutts! *Yah!*"

The dogs could not ignore this man's command. With a chorus of yelps and snarls, they retreated back down the narrow lane and out to the main street. Emily's sandy-haired, twenty-something rescuer watched with a wide grin on his face before he turned and bowed.

"J.D. Roper at your service, *mademoiselle.*" The accent was obviously American, his clothes rumpled. "Senior correspondent, *PM Magazine.*"

PM Magazine? As if Emily had heard of it in Jerusalem. Her mother read British magazines like *Woman's Weekly* or *The Lady*, but certainly nothing from America.

"Thank you, Mr. Roper." Emily straightened her dress and tried to catch her breath. Her fists throbbed with pain, but that hardly mattered now. "I . . . ah . . ."

"You're lost." He finished her sentence. "You're a little young to be wandering around the island of Cyprus on your own. Famagusta's a rough town. And you're lucky I have a way with canines."

"I do appreciate your kindness. But I know where I am."

His smile seemed sincere enough, but Emily felt strangely uneasy with this stranger. If she could just get out to the street, perhaps she could find Nick Papakostas the way she had intended. But first—she looked around her feet.

"Here you go." J.D. Roper bent down to pick up the note she had dropped, then held it out to her—but just out of reach. His eyes quickly scanned the message: *Ride to the camps Nicolaos Papakostas.*

"Going my way, Miss—?"

"Emily Parkinson. Pleased to meet you." She snatched the note back, thought for a moment, then added for safety, "My father is Major Alan Parkinson. Perhaps you've heard of him."

J.D.'s eyebrows arched with sudden interest. "No kidding? Your pop's army brass? Here on Cyprus?"

"Jerusalem." Emily tried to brush by him. The sooner she got out of this wretched alley, the better.

"Oh, so you're here on vacation. Or what you Brits call a 'holiday.' "

"I'm on my way back to England, Mr. Roper. And I'm only here because my ship was asked to pick up some refugees, hardly a day out of Haifa harbor. Once we reached Cyprus, we were delayed with mechanical problems."

"Yeah, I heard all about that. The *Helgefjord,* right? Engines went belly-up. You'll be here for weeks before they get that tub fixed."

"Perhaps. But in the meantime—"

"In the meantime you're exploring alleys. And you're headed out to the camps?"

Emily tried to ignore the question.

"Thank you again for frightening the dogs away, Mr. Roper. I would have been fine in any case, however."

"Sure you woulda. Those little doggies looked nice and friendly."

She knew he was right. Sarcastic, but right. She realized her heart was still pounding in her chest from the near attack. Even so, she held her head high and walked as quickly as she could for the street.

"I must go. I'm looking for someone," she told him over her

shoulder. "Er . . . out in the camps."

Emily bit her tongue. Why had she said that? She didn't stop when he jogged up behind her.

"No kidding?" J.D. asked. "That's perfect!"

Perfection was hardly what Emily had in mind at the moment. She just wanted to get out of there.

But the American wasn't finished. "Look, miss. I'm here all the way from New York. Doing a story on the camps—you know, what's going on behind the barbed wire. People back home are interested. They can hardly believe our friends the Brits are holding all those Jewish refugees. No offense, miss, but it's a great story."

Emily frowned, but the idea occurred to her: Would this man know a way into the camps?

He kept up beside her. "It's like this. I'm . . . ah . . . I'm having a hard time getting past those camp guards. All I want to do is talk to a few folks, maybe snap a few shots. Is that such a big thing to ask? But those guards are stonewalling me. 'I'm sorry, sir.'" The American puckered his face and did a poor imitation of a British soldier. "'That's highly irregular.'"

Emily tried not to smile. "I'm sure they're just doing their jobs."

"Sure. But listen, maybe those fellas wouldn't say no to me so quickly if you were along to sweet-talk 'em a little. Strength in numbers. We both get in."

Emily thought for just a moment. No, it would never do. If she was going to get into the camps, she would do it on her own. Not at the side of J.D. Roper.

Emily started to walk away again, but not before J.D. had pushed a card into her hand.

"I'm staying at the Savoy Hotel. Leave me a message when you're ready to go, okay?"

She studied the card for a moment. *J.D. Roper, Senior Correspondent.*

"I'm honestly not sure I can help you. But I'll . . . I'll see what I can do."

That wasn't likely to be much. She hadn't even found Nick Papakostas yet. And she certainly didn't want to explain him and her plan to J.D. Roper. She hurried away.

"Emily!" Constance Pettibone held on to her skirt as she came around the corner. "We've been looking all over for you. *I've* been looking all over. Where have you *been?*"

"Oh, Miss Pettibone—"

Miss Pettibone looked the part of the proper English nanny— only young and slim, with a porcelain complexion. And her wide-eyed expression was the perfect explanation for Emily's secret nickname for her: Bambi.

"That gentleman at the restaurant was about to insist we have yet *another* portion of those horrid tree-leaf meatballs," she gasped, "and then I looked around, and you had simply *disappeared.* Honestly, you gave me a fright."

"*Koupepia.*" When J.D. Roper stepped up behind Emily, Miss Pettibone nearly jumped a foot in the air.

She recovered quickly. "I beg your pardon?"

"Kou-*pep*-ia," he repeated. "Stuffed vine leaves filled with aromatic steamed rice and spices. I had some last night, along with the grilled lamb on skewers. *Souvlaki,* I think the Cypriots call it. Delicious."

"And you are?"

Again the bow, again the introduction, again the New York address. After her initial fright, Miss Pettibone looked quite impressed. Her voice even twittered up an octave higher than when she spoke to Emily.

A sure warning sign.

"I'm Emily's governess, Constance Pettibone," she explained, as if she had met a long-lost friend on the voyage. "Actually, I was first hired as Emily's tutor, until her father asked me to accompany her home to England."

"A lovely name." He didn't let go of her hand as soon as he should have.

Emily groaned, though not loudly enough for anyone else to hear. Maybe the American could help her find Dov's mother; maybe he couldn't. Either way, she had a sinking feeling they would be seeing more of J.D. Roper.

A DOZEN MORE

3

"What are you two staring at?" Reb Herschel wanted to know.

"Someone's out there, Uncle." Golda leaned out the door of the Lieberman apartment.

"Golda! No!" Reb Herschel was at the door in a blink, holding his niece back. But the light from their door had brought the courtyard shadows to life.

Dov could only stare, slack-jawed, as they came closer.

"They're all girls," Golda whispered.

"What do you mean, all girls?" Dov took a closer look. He had an easier time imagining they were invading soldiers.

But girls?

"I see them, too." By that time Haviva had crowded the open door. Naomi too. So they all stood staring as a new attack began to rain down near them.

"Close the door!" cried Mrs. Elazar.

Her brother-in-law swept them back and stepped outside. "You!" he yelled to the shadows. "Children! Over here!"

"Herschel, please," his sister-in-law pleaded. "It's dangerous out there." But there was no going back.

"I'm coming with you," Dov said, and the man didn't say no. Together, they sprinted out into the damp night air, chasing shadows as a new wave of attacks whistled and thundered over their heads.

Dov was the first to come upon them. "Come with us." Dov thought he was taking one person by the arm, but four more emerged from the dark doorway, then six. Dark-eyed, dark-haired, dirty and barefoot, they couldn't have been much older than Golda or Haviva. But they seemed to guard themselves the way wild animals would, with one foot forward and one foot back, ready to retreat into the shadows at any time.

"Looks like we have a few more." Reb Herschel checked around the corner of a building.

For a moment Dov saw in their wide-eyed fright something he had seen before. He had lived it himself, then buried it in a deep part of his memory—a part of his memory he never wanted to uncover.

"Where are your parents?" asked Reb Herschel. But soon the answer to such a question was plain, even though the girls said nothing. Frozen in place, only their eyes darted left and right with the look of a hunted animal.

"No parents." Dov knew he wasn't telling Reb Herschel anything he didn't already suspect. The girls' faces—their eyes—told him everything.

Reb Herschel grunted. "You're from an orphanage somewhere, right? Weingartens' maybe?"

Another volley of shrieking bullets landed just behind them. Probably another direct hit to the Elazar home—and to Dov's radio equipment.

I should have taken it with me, Dov scolded himself, though he knew he couldn't have, not when he was helping Golda and Haviva.

Reb Herschel sighed. "Someone needs to answer me, girls. Where's Reuben Weingarten? Mrs. Weingarten?"

No one wanted to tell him.

"All right," he said. "We'll find out when we get them to safety. Doesn't the Torah say that the Holy One, blessed be His name, defends the fatherless? We should do the same."

That did sound like something in the Scriptures. Even here and now, Dov knew what was coming next.

"Where is it written, Dov?"

"Uhh . . ." Just now? Dov scanned the square for a safe way back as he searched his memory for an answer that might sound right. "The prophet?"

That brought a nod. Good. This was an odd place for a *yeshiva* school lesson, though.

"And which prophet?" Reb Herschel gathered the girls together as he spoke, readying them to run for cover.

How many prophets are there? "Jeremiah?" Dov guessed.

"Isaiah. You have some work to do. But first—" Reb Herschel waved his hand at the new refugees. "Are there more of you?"

Again, no answer. A few of the girls looked around, maybe to see if anyone was going to speak. Then Dov had an idea. He fished in his pocket to pull out the snack he'd offered Golda back in the Elazar living room.

"Here, you want a crab apple?" He held out the blotchy red-and-yellow fruit. It wasn't much of an offering, but the nearest girl snatched it out of his hand and instantly began stuffing it into her mouth.

"Ah, looks as if we've found something they like." Reb Herschel leaned closer to them, then pointed back at the Lieberman apartment. "You see that home over there? That's where we're going. You just have to come with us."

"You want more apples?" Dov asked them.

Finally one of the girls spoke up.

"I do."

"Good." Dov smiled and quickly started back across the hard-packed dirt of the Batei Machse Square. "So do I. Let's go see what we can find."

Reb Herschel and Dov hurried their troop of girls across the square, double time.

"Keep going," warned Reb Herschel as another *pop* of gunfire made Dov's ears ring. The girls didn't even seem to notice.

A moment later they all crowded into the apartment.

"We brought more visitors!" boomed the man, facing his hosts.

"One, two . . ." Naomi began to count.

"Ooo!" squealed Haviva. "Now we'll have a lot more kids to play Kick the Can with!"

Golda turned to the girl nearest her. "You *do* know how to play Kick the Can, don't you?"

"No."

"Well, then," Golda told her. "We'll teach you."

". . . eight, nine . . ." Naomi was still counting. And the girls still came out of the shadows.

"How many?" Old Mr. Lieberman's eyes grew.

"Come in, come in!" cried Mrs. Lieberman, wiping her hands on her apron. But she was blocked in the narrow hallway leading out of her kitchen. "Everyone is welcome. . . ." Her voice trailed off at the sight of so many little girls.

". . . ten, eleven . . ." Naomi tallied them up.

"Oh," was all Mrs. Lieberman could manage. At least the gunfire had now quieted.

Mr. Lieberman poked his head outside. "So, anyone else want to join us? How about you, Mrs. Goldstein? You've been watching the whole parade. You don't happen to have any extra blankets, do you? We've got a dozen orphans visiting. You tell me where they'll be sleeping, eh?"

A shutter slammed somewhere down the lane, and Mr. Lieberman chuckled dryly at his own dark humor.

"I don't know where you girls came from," he said, pulling the door shut. "And I certainly don't know how we're going to feed so many mouths. But you're welcome in our little home. At least for tonight."

"I'm sorry, Abraham." Reb Herschel shook his head at their new host. "It's getting far too dangerous out there. We have no choice but to bring them in."

"Of course, of course." The old man nodded and smiled. "I believe it's written somewhere that 'Sorrow shared is sorrow halved.' "

Reb Herschel rubbed his beard. "I'm afraid in this case we have sorrow times twelve."

"What happened to your teachers, dear one?" Mrs. Elazar gently held the chin and looked into the eyes of one of the older girls. "Do you want an apple?"

The orphan looked up hopefully.

"I think they're from the Weingarten Orphanage." Reb Herschel peeked out the door. "They're too afraid to tell me anything. But as soon as it has been quiet out there for a while, I'm going to go out and check."

"And I'll go with you," Dov added.

"Herschel." Mrs. Elazar wasn't so sure. "You don't think the Weingartens are—"

But her brother-in-law stopped her question with a shake of his head. Why else would the orphans have come searching for help?

She looked around at the crowd, and her eyes found Dov. "Perhaps Natan will be able to tell us what happened. He was here for a moment while you were gone, you know."

Dov perked up at the news, only to realize Natan was no longer in the impossibly crowded apartment.

"He brought your radio transmitter," Mrs. Elazar announced.

The radio! Dov had almost forgotten.

STRANDED

4

"Oh, *there* you are!" Constance Pettibone blinked her long eye-lashes and peeked out at where Emily sat in a torn canvas deck chair. Golden morning sunshine already washed the salt-stained wooden deck. "I was afraid you had run off to that dreadful island by yourself again."

"Not at all, Miss Pettibone." Emily stood up and spread out her hands as if she hadn't a care in the world. "I've been on board since yesterday."

"As well you should have been." Miss Pettibone's pout must have been perfected during years of eating very sour grapes. Or perhaps she was growing into her new job as governess. She ventured out on deck, one foot at a time. "I would not want to have to inform your parents that you had been attacked or injured in a dark alleyway." She shivered.

"I don't mean to be difficult, but don't you think you're being a bit melodramatic? I'm quite safe, you know."

"Safe? Hmph." The pout transformed into a frown. "Not if you insist on traipsing about this horrid island by yourself."

"I wouldn't call it 'traipsing.'" Emily leaned out over the rail and watched men loading crates of sweet-smelling oranges onto the tramp steamer behind them. Her mouth watered at the thought of how the oranges might taste.

"Well, then." Miss Pettibone went on. "What would you call what you were doing back in that dreadful alley yesterday?"

The question yanked Emily back to the present. She tried to think of a way to answer it without lying.

"Well, you see . . ."

It would take too long to explain about Mr. Nick Papakostas and how he was related to the friendly dock worker, Spiro Theodop . . . The Greek last names were terribly long and hard for an English girl to repeat.

"Yes?" Miss Pettibone raised her eyebrows.

How can I possibly tell her?

No, it would take too long to explain why Emily had taken on this odd bit of detective work. *I had this Jewish friend back in Jerusalem,* she might say. Miss Pettibone would then probably stare blankly at her with those big Bambi eyes, just as she always did.

And this friend somehow survived the Nazi work camps and has been searching for his missing family. And now, since his father died here, it seems there's a small chance his mother could be held in one of the British detention camps here on Cyprus.

The more Emily thought about it, the less her search made sense.

"Emily?"

And since we've taken a detour to Cyprus, why not try to find out what I can?

Though visiting a refugee camp sounded about as enjoyable as having teeth pulled, it was an opportunity she could not now pass up.

"I was just . . ." she began again, but the truth sounded too much like the plot to an impossible adventure novel. She only wished she could turn to the last page of the book to peek at how this story ended. Could she ever expect to find any word of Dov Zalinski's mother among the thousands of Jewish refugees behind barbed wire in the Cyprus camps? And was it really her concern?

It is, and I must!

But Emily couldn't explain that to Miss Pettibone. Not yet.

Emily cleared her throat. "I was lost."

Which happened to be quite true. On the other hand, it would take hours to explain Emily's growing conviction that she had arrived on this island not by accident, but for a definite reason.

And was it an accident how just this morning she had reached the part in her Bible about the apostle Paul's journey to Cyprus? There it was in the Acts of the Apostles, chapter thirteen.

She thought for only an instant. That was no accident, either. She had simply been reading and praying as she did most every morning, and chapter thirteen had followed chapter twelve, which followed chapter eleven. Perhaps God *had* brought her to Cyprus for a reason.

But why? To find Dov's mother? His father had died; she knew that much. But no one had ever been able to tell her or Dov anything about Mrs. Zalinski. Maybe the answer was one Emily didn't really want to know. The thought of searching the dreadful camps of half-starved war survivors made her shiver.

But she *had* promised Dov she would try to find out more about his mother. She could not escape the pledge.

There seemed to be no way to explain all this to Miss Pettibone, who had smiled at the sight of Emily's Bible and said, "How quaint."

Quaint, indeed!

Still, one look at her tutor told Emily Miss Pettibone wasn't satisfied by her short answer. She went on.

"I would have left the alley, but there were three horribly hungry-looking stray dogs"—Emily pulled back her own lip for effect—"with these horrible yellow teeth. They were coming straight at me. I expect they all had a terrible case of rabies."

"Oh dear." Miss Pettibone's eyes were wide. "Rabies?"

"To be truthful, I don't know about that part." Emily shrugged, then held up her finger as a storyteller would. "But I *can* tell you they had me cornered until that American, that Mr. . . . What was his name?"

"Roper." Miss Pettibone shielded a faint smile with her hand, but too late. "Jonathan Roper."

"Oh, *Jonathan*," answered Emily. This was something new. There was no mistaking the sickly sweet swoon in Bambi's voice. "He introduced himself to me as J.D."

"Did he?" Miss Pettibone sounded surprised and oh so innocent. "Is *that* who you joined last night for dinner?"

Miss Pettibone's cheeks flushed to crimson this time, but she recovered soon enough.

"Never you mind. But that reminds me." She fished a telegram out of her little black purse, and it flapped like a flag in the early-morning breeze off Famagusta Bay. "This came last night just after dinner. From your father."

"Oh!" Emily bit her tongue when she caught sight of the words *Palestine Command* on the heading. "From Daddy?"

Miss Pettibone smiled and held the thin telegram closer.

"Actually, it was addressed to me."

"Is everything all right?"

"Quite all right, I suppose. It seems to have been sent from Haifa for some reason, but he doesn't say anything about your mother or him."

Miss Pettibone was obviously enjoying her new position as telegram reader and news bringer.

"Then . . . what does it say?"

Miss Pettibone took a deep breath. " 'Remain Cyprus until I send airplane from Rome, stop.' "

She didn't need to read the word "stop" out loud after each sentence. But that was the way telegrams went.

" 'Expect arrival ten days, stop.' "

"Nearly two weeks until a plane arrives." Emily sighed. "Then we're quite marooned here."

"Quite." Miss Pettibone agreed.

So we agree on something! Emily gazed out across the awakening harbor. She wondered why Miss Pettibone remained until she saw who had just appeared on the pier below.

Miss Pettibone noticed, as well, and let out a little squeal as she checked her watch.

"He's early!" She held her hands to her head. "Oh, my hair is still a mess. And I'm not even—tell him I'll be right back, please. And do not allow him to leave. Under no circumstances!"

Emily could hardly keep from frowning as J.D. Roper—Jonathan—mounted the gangway up to the deck. But he brightened when he saw her leaning against the railing, her arms crossed.

"Well, good morning!" he boomed.

Emily did her best to smile as he looked past her shoulder.

"She's in powdering her nose. She asked if you might wait for a moment."

"What? Oh, you mean your governess?" J.D. Roper was not a very good actor. They stood on the deck for a moment, neither one speaking.

Finally Emily decided she might as well ask. "How is your story coming?"

He pointed at her as if he'd just come up with a great idea. "Good thing I found you here. I've been meaning to talk to you about that."

"So you haven't made it into the camp yet?" They had that much in common.

"You know those Brits." He laughed. "Always another form to

fill out, another '*shed-*ule' to match. They don't seem to get the fact that I came all the way from New York City for this. And I'm not leaving until I . . ."

His voice trailed off, and Emily turned to see what he was looking at. She could have guessed.

"Well." He smiled. Emily thought he looked goggle-eyed. "Ready to go?"

"You remembered." Constance Pettibone fluttered her eyelashes at her red shoes. Emily's stomach turned. "Emily, you'll be all right while I'm gone?"

"Oh, of course. I'll stay on the island the way Father said."

Emily wasn't sure if Miss Pettibone heard her. But as Miss Pettibone and J.D. turned to leave, there was no mistaking Spiro's shout from down below.

"Miss Emily!" He must have caught sight of her on the deck. "I talk to my cousin—you remember, the vegetable seller?"

"I'll be right down." Emily hurried for the ramp before he said anything else. Of course, J.D. probably already had his reporter's notebook ready. His instincts were too good to let this sort of thing pass.

"He said he would take you to the camp tomorrow morning. First thing." The burly dock worker held out his rough hands, and a bright white smile spread across his face. "Just what you wanted, no? Although, why a pretty girl like you would want to go to a place like that, I do not understand. I would watch myself in such a place."

By that time everyone in the harbor had probably heard Spiro. And Emily didn't dare look behind her to see if Miss Pettibone and her new beau had followed her down to the pier.

"His name is Papakostas, remember. Nick Papakostas."

Emily smiled. "That's wonderful, Spiro. Perfect."

Perfect, maybe. But no longer a secret.

MIPI OLALIM

5

"What is it you're hoping to do with that thing, exactly?" Old Mrs. Lieberman looked up from stirring a pot of thin lentil soup the next day. Dov had managed to string up his antenna wire from one side of the tiny kitchen to the other. He tried adjusting a couple of knobs on the transmitter, but through the earphones he could hear nothing but static.

"People need to know what's happening here, Mrs. Lieberman. If the world hears, they'll help us."

"You know this for a fact?"

"Well . . . sure. I think so."

Dov nodded as if he *was* sure of himself. Wasn't that what Emily's uncle Anthony always said? Tell the world! Make a difference with the truth. Anthony had even called it "the artillery of words."

"Hmm." Mrs. Lieberman didn't look too sure.

Dov couldn't tell from her expression if she approved, disapproved, or even understood. To tell the truth he wasn't quite sure himself, either. But he *was* sure that once he spouted such a lofty-sounding thing, everyone within shouting distance would probably hear. Here in the Liebermans' apartment, no one could speak in private.

Case in point: While Dov fiddled with the radio, Reb Herschel stood in the corner of the kitchen, waving his arms and arguing with Natan about the Irgun.

Natan's radical Irgun friends were too cold-blooded, insisted Reb Herschel. Terrorists, even.

No, they weren't. Yes, they most certainly were. Back and forth they argued. Natan said something about the Irgun taking the lead in the fight against the British, instead of letting the British push them around.

And while both men sounded as if they were trying to whisper, in this cramped space even their whispers resounded. The argument heated up even more when it came to defending the Old City.

"Forget about Irgun or Haganah," hissed Reb Herschel. "We are all in this together now. And I am still here, as you can see. My family will remain with me. My nephew Shimon, he is fighting, too."

"Ah, but if you could have left, you would have, isn't that so?"

"You're in the Irgun, and you ask me this? I thought the Irgun didn't *want* us around. Women and children just get in the way."

"Did I say that?" Natan ran his fingers through his black hair.

"That's what your leaders have told us, over and over."

"The leaders, perhaps, but not me. I say we need fighters, we need weapons, and we need someone to defend. Families or orphans, it doesn't matter."

"Ah yes, the orphans." Reb Herschel suddenly looked as if a heavy weight had fallen on his shoulders. "Have you heard about the Weingartens?"

Natan shook his head no, and Reb Herschel took a deep breath. Their argument had come to a screeching halt.

"They're gone," Reb Herschel said, looking at the ground.

"Gone?"

"I checked the orphanage this morning—or what's left of it. I don't see how anyone survived, much less a dozen children."

"They're survivors." Natan had the look of a survivor himself, with the determined glint in his eye and the set of his jaw. He adjusted an ancient-looking rifle he had taken out from underneath his thin coat and slung it over his shoulder.

"But you don't understand, Natan. This neighborhood is no place for children without parents. They need to be taken where there are no Arab bullets or attacks every night. Somewhere safe."

Under Mrs. Elazar's watchful eye, the children had spilled out into the small patio around the front door. But instead of playing the way normal children might, they huddled in small groups and whispered to each other. They knew firsthand about the attacks Reb Herschel spoke of.

"Somewhere safe?" Natan scowled. "And where might that be? The Arabs are attacking the Jewish Quarter here and the *Talbiya* neighborhood out there. Outside the walls, inside the walls—there is no safe place for a Jew. We're all targets."

"Perhaps true. And look, I appreciate your bravery." Reb Herschel seemed to soften. "But . . . you're not married. You don't have children. If you did, you would see things differently."

"Oh, come on." Natan forgot to whisper this time as he rolled his eyes. "I'm here in the Old City risking my life for you people. My comrades and I expect to have something—someone—to defend. I hope it's more than just you and—"

"I know a way to help the orphans escape," Dov put in. Neither man looked at him.

"The tunnel, Natan. We could clear some of the mess and get them back out through the tunnel!"

"Who asked?" snapped Natan, but Reb Herschel raised his hand.

"We should listen to the boy. What tunnel are you talking about, Dov?"

Dov stepped up to explain about Bin-Jazzi's tunnel, the one he and Natan had used to get into the Jewish Quarter only a few days before. But when he told them the plan that had just occurred to him, Natan shook his head and mumbled under his breath.

"You forget one thing." He sighed, pushing back his unruly hair.

"What's that?"

"The tunnel begins in an Arab neighborhood."

True. Why did Natan have to remind him like that?

"It was just an idea."

"Yes, well, the only thing you need to worry about is staying here in the Old City for now."

What choice did they have? The British hadn't let anyone out for days.

Natan headed for the door and looked out at the neighborhood.

"How's the transmitter coming, Dov?"

"I've almost got it going again."

"You sure you don't want to drill with the rest of us? We need all the help we can get."

Dov didn't answer his brother's second question. Drilling, marching around, and practicing soldiering skills only made him remember the Nazi camps—of the last war. And that was not something he wanted to remember.

He'd seen the young Jewish soldiers-to-be practicing around the fringes of the Machse Square, as if this war-to-be were a game. Some of the older ones even gripped real guns, half-hidden under shirts or behind their backs. Who knew if the weapons could actually fire. Others held sticks—which would do them a lot of good against Arab soldiers.

"Not yet, Nathan." Dov shook his head. "Maybe—"

"No, forget it. Forget I said anything. We need men. You haven't grown up yet."

"You can't say that!"

But he had. Natan marched out without another word.

A few hours later Dov held the microphone up to the young orphan girl. Kiva Moscowitz was probably eight or nine, though her eyes looked like those of an old woman.

"You don't speak Hebrew yet, do you?" he asked her.

Kiva shook her head. Like Dov, she had been born in Poland.

"That's okay." Dov did his best to sound grown-up, but his voice squeaked. "You'll learn. Just remember we're on the radio and no one can see you. Say everything so people will hear. Don't shake your head or anything like that. Got it?"

Kiva gulped and nodded.

"You can tell us in Yiddish. People will understand. So tell me, Kiva, where did your family come from?"

After a deep breath the girl opened her mouth and started into her story. She remembered the fires in Warsaw, the bombs, the people running. She told of hiding, of the soldiers who chased them, and of coming to Palestine with some distant relatives who had made her beg for food. That was before they disappeared one morning, too.

"And the rest of your family?" A knot started to form in Dov's throat. He already knew the answer to that question. "What happened to your parents?"

Kiva could only shake her head; for the listeners, the silence was answer enough.

"You did a good job, Kiva," he told her. And he knew that if he said much of anything else, he would choke up. Her story made him remember, and it hurt.

Chava Bazak came next.

"Last year for my birthday, my *abba* gave me this *siddur*," she told Dov. She clutched her beautiful black prayer book as if it were a lifesaver, and she on a sinking raft. Maybe she was. Maybe they all were. "I thought it was like a treasure. And I would take it with me every *Shabbat*, when we all walked to the Hurva Synagogue, before . . . before . . ."

That was as far as Chava Bazak went before her eyes filled with tears and her voice trailed away into her memories. She sat with the siddur clutched tightly to her chest, rocking. Her sad brown eyes told Dov the rest of the story. But who could hear it on the radio?

She had been right about the siddur. It was a treasure.

Mipi Olalim, it read in gold letters across the front cover.

From the mouths of babes.

Chava seemed to pull back the tears when Dov waved for someone else to come in. She tucked the siddur under her arm and hurried off. Next?

Frieda Horowitz was a little better; she managed to get through five or six questions before she, too, started crying. But after what she told them, who could blame her?

And then there was little Batya, who couldn't tell Dov her last name. Did she even know it? It made him feel older to hold a microphone in his hand and ask questions, just as Anthony would do. But by that time Dov was wondering, *For this radio program I risked my life?*

"They told me I never had a mother and father," explained

Batya, her voice quivering. "And that I never would. Do you think that's true?"

Dov opened his eyes to see her staring at him with dark eyes that had seen far too much. What should he tell her?

"No. That's not true." Dov surprised even himself with his words. "You'll have a mother and father someday."

What had made him say that?

Batya smiled and seemed to believe him. "Just like you, right?"

"That's right. Just like me."

Satisfied, she skipped off to join the others. Dov hoped she would forget his words as quickly as she had believed them.

"This is another special broadcast of the *Kol Hamegen Haivri*, the broadcasting service of the Haganah, coming to you from the Jewish Quarter of the Old City." Dov sighed when he finished his fourth and last interview. He knew he couldn't handle any more. "These are the voices of the people who are trapped in this city. These are the people under attack."

He switched his radio transmitter to the standby setting, only to see the yellow-lit dial flicker. He guessed his battery had only a few short minutes of power left.

So much for that.

For once he was alone in the tiny Lieberman kitchen, and he used the time to stare at the transmitter.

"Is that hard?" asked someone from the doorway.

Dov jumped in his chair.

"Oh." Dov glanced back to see Natan. "Why do you always have to scare people like that?"

"I'm not scaring you. And why do you have to answer a question with another question? I asked you first."

"What?"

"Radio-broadcasting stuff. Is it, uh, hard to do?"

The question sounded strange, coming from his brother.

Dov shrugged. "I watched someone else do it. It's easy."

It was as simple as asking questions and pushing a microphone in someone's face. The hard part was listening to the words they had said, pretending that each one did not cut his heart.

"My parents are gone. . . ."

"When I came back, my parents had disappeared. . . ."

"The soldiers took my parents away. . . ."

Was this part of Anthony's "artillery of words"? If so, Dov would have to turn the cannon away from himself.

Who were they trying to reach this way? The British, who were leaving in a few weeks anyway? The Arabs? A war he could understand, but a weapon of words was something else. He glanced once more at the radio dial, then tapped it to make sure.

The dial was dark.

Dov flipped the main switch up and down a few more times, just to check. But he knew the battery was close to dead.

And as he sat thinking, Dov thought he heard a now-familiar shriek outside. The Lieberman house shuddered at the dull thud outside.

"There it is again!" yelled Mr. Lieberman. "Get all the children inside!"

But they didn't have a chance before an explosion rained dust and plaster on his head.

"No!" Dov hardly had a chance to duck.

NICK PAPAKOSTAS

6

"Where is that Mr. Papakostas?" Emily whispered to herself. She could see nothing unusual when she peeked over the ship's railing, down at the pier. No produce wagon, no vegetable truck. What had Spiro told her the day before? That his cousin would meet her first thing in the morning? She wondered if "first thing in the morning" meant something different here on Cyprus.

A tugboat out in the harbor was already working up a good head of steam, filling the fresh morning air with eye-watering coal smoke. Emily rubbed her eyes and wished the men on the *Desdemona* would sleep a little longer, just like Miss Pettibone.

Desdemona . . . Her mind wandered. *Isn't she a heroine in one of Shakespeare's plays?*

"Ahem." The Norwegian deckhand wasn't trying to startle her, but Emily nearly lost her footing as she shot to her feet. So much for Shakespeare.

"Er, just watching the harbor." She smiled. The blond young man scratched his head and stepped back.

"An American fellow has been waiting for you in the lounge, miss. A Mr.—"

"Roper?" Emily finished his sentence with a groan. Where had he come from? He must have sneaked aboard even before she came out on deck. "Is Miss Pettibone with him? How long has he been there?"

"He is alone." The deckhand shrugged. "And he's on his third cup of coffee. He asked me to check if you were out here."

"Thank you," Emily said. "But please tell Mr. Roper that I'm not here."

She caught herself. "No, I mean, tell him I'll be leaving shortly, that I don't have time to chat."

The deckhand didn't have a chance.

"Ah, *there* you are, Emily!" An oval door swung open, and the lanky American stepped out to join them. He wore khaki pants, a wrinkled white shirt, and a black press camera around his neck. "I've been waiting for you all morning."

Trapped! Emily wondered how she could get away from J.D. Roper now. At least Miss Pettibone wasn't on his arm.

"I'm sorry, Mr. Roper. I didn't realize we were supposed to meet. I have a busy day planned, I'm afraid."

"You bet we do. Don't you remember? I'm sure our ride to the camp'll be here in a minute."

Emily frowned. She didn't care for the way he said "we" and "our."

"But you don't understand. I'm afraid I cannot . . ."

"Hey, don't worry." He winked. "I told Constance I'd keep an eye on you. You're in good hands."

Emily backed away as her mind raced to think of something, anything to keep him from coming with her. But he had already set his hook. And then a wheezy horn sounded from down on the ~r, twice.

"Ah, that must be Mr. Papakostas." J.D. smiled and handed

his coffee cup to the deckhand before he hurried down the ramp to the pier.

Emily clenched her fists and followed. "Wait for me!" she called out.

But J.D. didn't seem to hear her as he jogged over to an ancient delivery truck perched at the edge of the pier, wheezing and puffing blue smoke. The back of the truck was piled high with canvas sacks bulging with potatoes, cabbages, and . . . Emily wasn't sure what else. A grinning man sat behind the wheel. Emily nearly stumbled, grabbed the gangplank handrailings with both hands, and hurried to catch up.

"Mr. Roper," she cried, "please!"

But by the time she stepped down to the pier, J.D. was already shaking hands with their smiling driver. The truck engine had finally shuddered to a halt.

"So you're the one who's going to take us to the camp, eh?" The American could pump hands as well as anyone.

"Nicolaos Papakostas, at your service," replied the other man. He flashed a gap-toothed smile below a salt-and-pepper mustache. Both ends were twisted to a jaunty point, Greek style. Emily thought he looked like something out of a travel poster for a holiday in Athens.

"J.D. Roper. You don't mind if I call you Nick, do you?"

"Not at all." Their driver tipped his floppy cap when he noticed Emily approach.

"This is my friend Emily Parkinson," announced J.D. as he stepped around to the passenger side. "She's the young detective who's searching for her relative."

Well, not quite *her* relative. But without waiting for an invitation, J.D. opened the door and slid into the front seat.

What else could she do? Emily found a place next to the window.

"Very pleased to meet you, Miss Emily Parkinson." Their driver never stopped smiling. "We go now?"

Emily nodded as Nick cranked the ignition to restart his truck. *Whirr-whirr-whirr* . . .

Nick paused a moment before he gently touched the small, round picture of a bearded saint mounted on the dashboard.

Why did he do that? wondered Emily.

He turned the key once more. *Vrooom!* The ancient engine finally roared back to life.

"I need one of those lucky charms for my typewriter," said J.D.

I don't think so. But Emily didn't want to be rude to their host.

Nick grinned as he arm-wrestled an oversized gear-shift knob into gear. Somehow he avoided J.D.'s knees. With a mighty grinding and popping, they lurched backward, turned, and headed back around the morning traffic of the harbor city.

"Now, Miss Parkinson." J.D. held on to the dashboard with one hand and pointed at her with the other. "I'm curious about your search, here. You're looking for *whom*, exactly?"

Emily paused as she tried to think of how much she should tell the American.

"A friend. Actually, the mother of a friend."

"That would be a *Jewish* friend, since we're going to the Larnaca camps? Someone from Jerusalem?"

Emily sighed. The man was a reporter, all right.

"His father made it to Cyprus, so there's a small chance that perhaps his mother did, too. I promised him I'd find out if I could."

"Ah, I see." J.D. nodded. "Constance said you seemed quite . . . intent."

"I don't think she understands. But I left her a note."

"That's good." He looked at his wristwatch.

"She should see it when she finally wakes up." Emily was

about to add something about how late Miss Pettibone had stayed out the night before but thought better of it.

"Er, what's that building over there?" J.D. cleared his throat as he changed the subject and turned to their driver.

Nick pointed to a large stone church keeping guard over the middle of the town. A Muslim minaret tower had been added to one of the tall, fortress-like square towers.

"Cathedral Saint Nicolas," he explained as they careened around another corner. "I was named for this saint, from fourteen century." He pointed once more to the picture on his dashboard, apparently of the long-gone church leader. "This building was turned to mosque in 1571."

Emily held on for her life as they jolted over an extra-deep pothole. Nick leaned on his horn as they barreled toward a dusty old man on a donkey. His English may not have been excellent, but in this British colony, everyone understood the language of the horn perfectly.

"Those beasts think they own the road." J.D. seemed to be enjoying the ride as they left the city behind and began snaking up a set of low, rock-studded hills. Nick tossed a friendly Greek comment out the window; the old man with the donkey returned his wave. And still they climbed, barely outrunning a thick cloud of dust.

Not far up the narrow road, they passed a tiny whitewashed stone church, its crooked walls displaying centuries of faithful care. Farther on, clusters of blue-green olive trees winked in the breeze, looking like the eyebrows of the hills. And in the distance a shepherd surrounded by dozens of his sheep watched them hurry by. He might have stepped out of a time machine, or he might have belonged to a flat-roofed little farmhouse they passed a few minutes later. As with the church, centuries had blurred the edges of the landscape, and straight lines seemed not to matter. The house had once been painted slate blue to match the sky, but the color had mellowed to a faded eggshell color, just as the rocky hills had faded.

But the old hills also showed off splashes of new color. Along the roadside they came upon thousands of daisies erupting in bright yellows and golds, floating on a pale purple sea of poppies. The wind from inland seemed to gently shake the carpet, sending ripples down the hills at them. Emily smiled and rolled down her window all the way to catch the sweet-spiced scent of pines and hay, flowers and oranges. In the distance a faint rumble hinted at rain.

"It's lovely." She did her best to take in the stark island countryside, all the way to the glittering blue sea in the distance behind them. "Simply lovely."

"Yes." Nick's face seemed to light up even more than the Mediterranean sun following them up the hill. He must have understood her wonder. "Bee-you-tea-fool, no? This is my beautiful island."

"You're very lucky to live here."

"Then you stay?"

"Pardon me?"

For the first time Emily was glad J.D. Roper sat between her and the friendly driver. Was this the way men on Cyprus talked, or did he have something else in mind? But the American laughed as if it were a joke. Maybe it was.

"Miss Parkinson's father is an important British army officer," J.D. explained. "I'm sure they have a fine home already, back in England. Right, Emily?"

Emily felt an elbow in her ribs.

"Naturally." She didn't know how to answer such an odd question.

"Too bad." Nick drove on over the crest of the hills. Higher up, a bank of dark clouds crouched in waiting for them.

"Is that rain up ahead?" Emily whispered.

"Rain, yes," answered Nick. "Rain, British camp, and mud."

Nick's predictions proved true a few minutes later, when, like muddy tears, the first drops found their cracked windshield. Tears turned to a steady downpour as they neared the camps.

"Headquarters Camp, three miles." J.D. read the neatly lettered sign, but Emily was the first to spot the low outline of barbed-wire fences and rounded metal Quonset huts up ahead, topped by a collection of spindly guard towers. For a moment they reminded her of tall spiders guarding the food they had caught in their barbed webs.

"Oh." She squinted and pointed through the rain. Nick's windshield wipers managed only to smear the dirt from one side to the other. "Is that it?"

"Dekalia Camp 70," announced Nick. He'd left his smile somewhere back in the daisy fields. A sodden-looking guard at the gate held up his hand for them to stop, while another checked his rifle from inside a small guardhouse. A heavy timber guardrail blocked their way in through a gap in the double barbed-wire fence.

"You're sure you want to go inside?" mumbled J.D.

"Are you?" Emily whispered back. The truck's brakes squealed as they rolled to a soggy stop in a gathering puddle. The guard ignored the soaking and glared in at them. Did he recognize Nick and his truck?

"Who are you?" he barked, looking past the driver.

"J.D. Roper, *PM Magazine*, New York, New York." J.D. leaned over and stretched his hand out the window. "Pleased to meet you."

The guard kept his arms crossed while a sheet of driving rain ran off the edge of his black beret and down his nose.

"Identification, Mr. Roper? What's your purpose here?"

"Ah, sure." While J.D. fished out his press card, he explained that he was doing an article on the camps and that his editor in New York was very interested in telling the British side of the story.

"And what about you?" The guard hadn't let J.D. finish his sales pitch. Instead, he stared straight at Emily.

He's not going to hurt me, she told herself. *Don't be silly.*

But she could not help shivering. And it occurred to her that maybe she should have stayed back on the ship after all.

PROVE IT

7

"Are you all right?" Natan gripped Dov's shoulder to keep him from shaking, but Dov could not seem to stop. At least the shelling was over for now. On their fourth full day in the Old City, they'd taken several more hits, but this time they had caused more mess than real damage.

Dov took a deep breath as they stood outside the Lieberman front door. It smelled of gunpowder, concrete dust, sweat, and fear. He tried to cover his nose, but still he had to breathe.

"Yeah. I'm okay. But the girls—"

"Get over it." Natan leaned against the side of the building and scanned the square. "Your orphans are fine."

"What do you mean, *my* orphans?"

"I mean they're the ones you're worried about. They made it this far, didn't they?"

"Sure. But there's been so much shooting."

"Shooting? Ha! Hasn't anyone told you the real fighting hasn't even begun?"

"That's what I keep hearing."

"It's true. Believe me."

"I don't know *what* to believe anymore."

Natan chuckled. "Now you're sounding like me."

"That's a scary thought." Dov kicked a stone as hard as he could. He tried not to hop with pain as it skittered across the packed dirt of the courtyard.

Was Dov starting to sound like his brother? If there was one person he did *not* want to imitate, it was Natan. Natan, who never smiled. Natan, who seemed as cold and faraway as the snow back on the Austrian Alps.

Now Dov wondered.

He's my brother, after all.

For a crazy moment Dov wondered if Natan might not be right in what he was doing. It was *something*, after all, as opposed to *nothing*.

"I'd better go." Natan turned to leave. "No time to chat."

"Wait a minute." Dov started to say something, changed his mind, then took a breath.

"What?"

"I was just wondering." Dov didn't look his brother in the eye. "Do you ever get tired of hiding from the British, waiting for something to happen?"

"I'm not waiting. I'm getting ready."

Dov looked for another rock to kick. "All the rest of us are doing is sitting here and waiting. Just once, I'd like to . . ."

Natan looked straight at him, his eyebrow twitching.

"I'd like to make something happen," Dov blurted out. "Or at least *help* make something happen. Do you know what I mean?"

Dov caught his breath. Where had that come from? It was probably the most he'd ever said to his brother at one time, and he could have kicked himself for saying it.

Natan studied him for a moment. "I think I know what you mean." When Natan smiled, it almost looked as if it hurt him.

Dov wasn't sure he had seen the ends of his brother's mouth turn up that way before. Perhaps he had borrowed the smile from someone, a temporary loan.

"Then can I ask you something else?" Dov asked.

Natan's curled-up eyebrow seemed to say yes. Dov would have to ask quickly. Surely the big-brother act couldn't last much longer.

"If someone told you they might look for our mother, do you think there might be a chance . . . of finding her?"

Natan squinted. "Where in the world did that come from?"

"It's something I've been thinking about. I have this . . . friend."

Emily Parkinson's promise still echoed in Dov's memory. *"If there's ever any way to find your family . . . perhaps even your mother . . . I'll do what I can."*

"Tell your crazy friend not to bother." Natan frowned. "Our mother died at Dachau."

"How do you know for certain? What if she were somehow alive? What then?"

"Do you know how many people died in those camps?"

More questions for answers.

"But *for certain*, Natan? Do you know *for certain*? My friend said—"

"And you believe what everyone tells you? What does he know, this friend?"

"She."

"Oh, a *girl*, even?" Natan laughed bitterly. "A girl is going to find our mother?"

"For your information, her father is . . ." Dov wasn't sure he could finish what he had begun to explain. "I mean, she knows certain people. She's English."

Something inside Natan must have snapped at the word.

"*Another* English friend?" Natan slammed the side of the

building with his fist. Clearly the big-brother moment had ended. "Look, I know a few of them are on our side. But only a few. You need to be more careful."

"What are you talking about?"

"Do I have to spell it out for you? Most English are two-faced liars who pretend to keep the peace, but only when it suits them and their Arab friends! They've strangled us! No better than Hitler, they are."

"I only meant—"

"I don't care what you meant." This was the old Natan again. Maybe the new, nice Natan had been an accidental visitor. "I wouldn't believe a single word from an English mouth. And you're a fool if you do."

"What about *Imma*? She grew up in England!"

"Our mother couldn't help where she was born."

Dov was silent for a moment, then said, "So you don't think she could be alive?"

"Not for a minute. And you're dreaming if you do."

"But what if she is?" Dov couldn't give up. Not yet. "What if my friend—"

"I'll bet your friend just wanted you to give her information or something."

"I don't think so."

"Prove it."

"I don't have to prove anything. You don't know what you're talking about."

"*I* don't? You're nuts." Natan wheeled on his heel and stomped off. "And I don't have to deal with this."

"Fine." Dov dug the toe of his shoe into the ground. "If you don't care, I'll find her myself."

For a moment Natan stopped in his tracks. "You're wasting

your time on a fantasy, Dov. I'm looking ahead. You're looking back."

"But—"

"And another thing!" he yelled, turning again to leave. "You're about the most gullible person I've ever met. You believe anything anyone tells you. Hear me? You're just . . ."

Dov didn't hear the rest of his brother's hot speech. He turned back inside, but he couldn't quite see the door; it swam in his vision until he wiped his eyes with his sleeve. Was he really wasting his time, hoping his mother might be alive? That their father was dead, buried in a British camp on Cyprus, he knew. But no one knew for sure about Imma. And no news could mean . . . well, why wouldn't Natan at least *listen* to him?

He tried to imagine how Natan might have treated him if he'd been trying to fight their war with a gun instead of with a silly shortwave radio transmitter.

Two girls rushed past him in a game of tag. One shouted, and Dov had to cover his ears.

Too many voices! And all of them shouting. Insisting.

Believe.

Don't believe.

Trust.

Don't trust.

Fight.

Wait.

Do the right thing.

Only, what *was* the right thing? Dov would have screamed if he hadn't been surrounded by strangers. Maybe it was just the difficulty of living with so many others in a tiny apartment, like a can of sardines, and probably smelling a lot worse.

"Natan," he called after his brother. "Wait."

Natan was well down the street by now, and not about to wait.

Even so, Dov ran after him. They ran block after block through the winding, deserted streets of the Old City.

"Natan. Stop! I want to help. Can't I do *something*?"

Something, *anything*—as long as it was with his brother. At least that would be better than sitting with all the others, waiting for bullets to rain down.

"We don't need crybabies to defend the neighborhood," mumbled Natan. "We need men."

"I'm a man."

"Nice try. I'll bet you haven't even held a gun before."

"I have, too." *What am I saying?*

"Where? Back in Poland?"

"No. Here in *Eretz* Israel. On a kibbutz farm."

Dov didn't dare explain that he had only held one old World War I rifle for a few seconds, before his friend Henrik had taken it from him.

Natan slowed down a little. "You a good shot?"

"I have a good eye, but I was thinking—"

"But what about the Haganah and your broadcasts?"

"The battery's almost dead. What else can I do with the transmitter? Throw it at the Arabs?"

"Maybe that's not such a bad idea."

Dov didn't much like the idea, and Natan chuckled in his own dry way. But still Natan didn't stop—nor did he stop Dov from following him through a large drainage pipe, down a set of stairs, and into the shadowy basement of a burned-out building.

Dov kept on Natan's heels, not fully knowing why. Maybe he could use a messenger, something like that.

"Where are we going, Natan?"

"Keep your mouth shut. I'll do the talking."

DEKALIA SEARCH

8

"If you want a job, Miss Parkinson, just come to New York." J.D. Roper flashed his brightest smile. "We'll find a place for you at *PM Magazine*, guaranteed."

"But I'm only going on fourteen, Mr. Roper. I hardly think—"

"Just joking." He hopped down out of the truck and turned back. "But seriously, you do have a way with words. I'll have to remember that line next time I want to get in someplace: 'My father is Major Alan Parkinson.' Open sesame! Welcome to Camp 70. Everybody bows!"

"Please. No one bowed. And I really don't care for the way you exaggerate."

"Whoa!" He held up his hands. "No offense. But the gates opened, didn't they?"

"That was only because they were expecting Mr. Papakostas to deliver his goods."

"Okay, but you gotta admit, you got their attention."

Emily supposed so. Maybe the guard thought she was an official visitor.

J.D. went on, as he seemed to like to do. "Hey, you take care of yourself, all right? Hope you don't mind."

That would mean he hoped she didn't mind that he was leaving them.

"Not at all. I'll be just fine." *In fact, I prefer to be without you.*

"I've got a story to write." He waved his hand at the camp. "And somewhere out there is a Pulitzer Prize with my name on it. I can see the headline now: 'J.D. Roper Wins Pulitzer With Brilliant Exposé of Conditions in Cyprus Camps.' "

He thumped on the truck's rusty fender and trotted for cover under the nearest tent. The rain had let up somewhat, but the camp was still dripping wet, and brick-red rivulets still coursed down hard-packed dirt roads.

"Hope you find who you're looking for!" J.D. shouted back at them as Nick ground the gears and jerked down the muddy road toward Emily's destination—the administration hut.

"Zalinski," repeated a bleary-eyed clerk behind a metal desk a few minutes later. "Leah Zalinski."

Emily waited as he pulled out first one file, then another. But each time he shook his head.

"Don't you have a list of some sort?" Emily tapped her toe, hoping the young soldier would see how serious she was.

"See here, Miss—"

"Parkinson. Emily Parkinson. My father is—"

"Yes, I know all that." The man tossed a heavy file her direction. "I suggest you take a look at that list."

Emily leaned forward. If he couldn't find the name, perhaps she could.

But her face fell when she got a closer look.

"Donald H. Duckman?" She looked up for an answer. "You can't be serious."

"Quite serious. Although the people giving us their names obviously were not. See here? There are plenty of others."

Emily didn't understand. "But why?"

"Stiff-necked. Uncooperative. Devious. These people don't like us. Shall I go on?"

"No. I understand you quite well enough."

"The American sailors who worked on the illegal ships were the most creative. We've caught a few of them, but there are still several out there trying to hide behind the skirts of these people. Cowards and criminals, if you ask me. And other refugees are illiterates who hardly even know their own names."

"Now, wait just a minute." The stormy expression on Emily's face didn't seem to shame the clerk, who shrugged and pulled his register back.

"You're welcome to look for your missing person on your own, if that's what you want. I'm just telling you that it's impossible to keep track of these people, especially when so few of them will cooperate with us. Maybe you should check in with the JDC."

He meant the Joint Distribution Committee, run by American Jews who had come to help manage most of the camp's day-to-day affairs.

"Perhaps I will." Emily sighed. "But first, could you look for a man named *Mordecai* Zalinski? I was told back in Jerusalem that he had died in one of these camps. Can you at least tell me where his grave might be?"

"Well, why didn't you say so right away? Finding a dead one could be a little easier. Although they don't speak to us any more willingly when they're dead than when they're alive."

He chuckled at his dark joke, but by that time Emily had just about had enough of the surly clerk. She turned on her heel and stepped for the door.

"Never mind. I'll be sure to tell my father how helpful you've been, Corporal . . ."

"Just call me Mouse. Corporal Mickey Mouse."

Emily slammed the door behind her, shutting out his annoying laughter. "I shan't be needing his help. I'll just find her on my own."

She marched out to the waiting truck, slid in, and slammed the door.

"We will find your mother," Nick told her in a quiet tone. He looked about as glad to be there as she felt—which wasn't very.

"Oh. It's not *my* mother. It's . . ." Emily didn't want to bore the man with the details, especially if he didn't understand English very well.

"Is *someone's* mother, is she not?"

Emily nodded. Perhaps Nick understood more than she thought.

"Then we find her, if she lives. This is no place for a mother."

Emily had to agree with his logic. This *was* no place for a mother. Or anyone else, for that matter.

"Even so, I'd feel a sight better if these prison officials would at least *try* to help."

Ahead of them, rounded metal Quonset huts seemed to march up the hills in neat British lines. They looked like huge ribbed tin pipes cut in half, lengthwise, and they rose out of the hard-packed yellow mud as far as Emily could see. Off on the fringes, several sad-looking olive-drab tent cities had been planted, as well. Emily wondered what it would be like to sleep in such a tent—especially if this rain didn't stop.

Whatever have I gotten myself into? she asked herself.

Nick whistled a Greek-sounding tune, but she noticed his eyes dart from left to right. Maybe it was just the sight of the no-nonsense, thirty-foot barbed-wire fence that hemmed them in on all sides. Twenty feet beyond the first fence, the British had planted another fence like the first.

Just to be sure. Emily imagined one of her father's officers laying out the design of this place on a neat sheet of yellow paper, drawing straight lines with a ruler, measuring out the distances exactly so. Every seventy-five yards, they'd plant a forty-foot-tall guard tower. Over here would be a water spigot, here the infirmary, and up there the mess hall.

Except the camp's occupants hadn't been designed with a straightedge ruler. Emily could feel the gaze of their hollow, sunken eyes as she and Nick passed slowly down the central lane. Most wore tattered clothes; many of the children went barefoot in the mud. When she looked up, they glanced away quickly.

"They don't look at us." Emily shivered. "Why don't they look at us?"

"No. They never do." Nick pointed to the back of a hut, doors open wide. "We are here. Stay by truck."

When the crowds began gathering around their truck, Emily understood why Nick had said that. A group of hard-faced men in Palestinian khaki took stations around them, their arms crossed and their backs to the truck. They were obviously not British, so they couldn't have weapons. But with the looks on their weathered faces, they wouldn't need any.

"This my potato guard." Nick jerked a thumb toward the forboding men and laughed as he hopped up into the back of his truck and began tossing down sacks to the waiting mess-hall crew. All around them a growing crowd of people watched every sack as if it were filled with gold.

Where had she seen such faces before? And then she remembered the day when her father had been called to handle a crowd of illegal immigrants, a shipful of desperate people who had landed in the Promised Land without official British permission. That was the day she met Dov. She remembered the dark faces, the blank eyes, the hollow cheeks.

Just like those in Camp 70.

Well. She took a deep breath and made up her mind. *I'm not going to find anyone sitting here in the truck.* So while Nick finished unloading, Emily slipped open the door and waded out into the crowd.

Would any of them know Dov's mother? How would she find out? No one seemed to speak the same language. She heard Polish and Romanian, a little Russian. Yiddish was mixed into the stew, as well. As for English? Probably not. But then again, many of the Jews in this crowd had to know Hebrew.

"Pardon me," she began. "I'm looking for a person who might be at this camp. The last name is Zalinski. From Warsaw."

A tired-looking young woman holding a small child glanced at her with the same haunted look of fear Emily had seen before.

"Do you speak English?" Emily stooped to catch the woman's eye. "Hebrew?"

The woman shook her head and pulled back into the shadows of her tin hut.

"No, I don't suppose you do." Emily squared her shoulders and headed for the next hut.

How long can this take? she asked herself. *There are what, ten thousand refugees in this camp? And none of them can talk to each other . . . let alone to me.*

Emily tried not to think of how impossible her task seemed, and she wished her Yiddish were better. She prayed quietly as she went from door to door, through the mud.

"If Mrs. Zalinski is alive, dear God," she whispered, "please let me find her somehow."

THE TEST

9

As Dov's eyes got used to the darkness, a dozen shapes melted out of the shadows.

"So," growled a low voice, "you brought your kid brother to play?"

Dov felt the hair on the back of his neck stand up.

"You're not going to talk about me like that," Dov began. "I—"

But he didn't have time to argue. He gasped at a blow to his chest.

"He wants to help, Asher," explained Natan. "He's pretty tough. We need the men."

"Men, yes," replied another of the shadows. "Not boys who like playing with radios."

Dov would have said something back, but he was still gasping for air.

Asher laughed. "All right, give him your gun, Menahem. Let's see if he can handle one of these things."

A moment later someone pressed a rifle into Dov's hands. It

felt colder than he expected, oily to the touch, and not at all pleasant.

"Are you ready to use one of these?" asked Asher. "Ready to kill any Arab who sets foot in this neighborhood? Ready to defend Eretz Israel?"

"Wait. I'm . . ." Dov's voice faded. Suddenly following Natan to this place didn't seem like such a grand idea. What had he gotten himself into?

"What did you say?" Asher pressed in from the side. His breath felt hot on Dov's cheek. "Let me hear you say it."

"I'm sure," Dov finally managed, though it sounded like the squeak of a mouse. Sure of *what*, he couldn't say.

"*Louder!*"

"I'm *sure*!"

Sure that he was out of his mind to be here doing this. Who was he kidding?

"All right." Natan's friend seemed satisfied, at least for the moment. "Let me see you aim at that window. Put it up to your shoulder. Watch the trigger, though. The safety doesn't always work, and that thing is loaded."

"Listen, I don't think—" Dov began.

"Do it!" barked Asher.

Dov tried to concentrate on what Asher told him. But all he could think of was his Arab friend, Mr. Bin-Jazzi—the man who had taken him into his shop and fed him. The man who had told him about Jesus and not hating people—any people. What would Mr. Bin-Jazzi have said if he were here now?

Dov heard rocks crumbling behind them, and a cry.

His heart leaped. "Who's there?" he shouted.

He swung the rifle around and felt the muzzle hit someone in the half darkness. The flash and explosion threw him backward in an instant—hardly time to realize he was shooting in the dark. The next moment he tumbled onto his back in the rubble.

What have I done?

"No!" Dov got up from the rubble of the basement hideout, straining his eyes to see if he had shot anyone with Menahem's greasy rifle. He prayed desperately that he had not. The shot echoed in his ears, along with horrible shouting and screaming.

"Down! Down!" yelled Asher. "We're under attack!"

"No, we're not. I see someone. Over there!" Natan scrambled to the corner, chasing an intruder. A pile of bricks tumbled to the ground. At least Natan was still alive. And just when Dov thought everyone in the dark room was safe, he heard a wailing scream, like that of a wild animal caught in a trap.

"Ay-eeEEEE!" The wailing brought a flash of light. A flashlight lit up a pair of frightened eyes for a split second. The scream pierced the chaos Dov's shot had ignited.

"Ow!" This time Natan howled. In the confusion Dov could see his older brother trying to tame a squirming, wailing animal by sitting on top of it. But the animal would not be tamed so easily.

Gladly leaving the rifle behind, Dov leaped to help. But all he got was a heel slamming into his cheekbone.

"Ohh!" Dov's face erupted in pain, but there wasn't time to worry about it. He grabbed again at the animal's legs.

Or rather, the little girl's legs. His hand brushed against the hem of a dress.

"Let me go let me go let me go," she cried in Polish. "Help me, Dov! Don't let them hurt me!"

Dov backed off at the sound of his name. It was Kiva, the first orphan he had interviewed for his broadcast. The young Polish girl.

"Let her go," he commanded his brother, pulling Natan by the shoulder. "I said, let her go!"

The words momentarily stunned Natan into silence.

"What are you doing? Do you know her?" Menahem asked. Now they all stood around the intruder.

Dov helped Kiva to her feet, and she looked up at him with saucer eyes.

"I just came to see where you went, Dov," she whispered. "We were worried about you."

"A friend of yours?" scoffed Asher. He turned to Natan. The light from his flashlight betrayed his expression—as if someone had just told a ridiculous joke. Natan could only shrug as he stuttered for a way to explain his younger brother.

"You need to leave," snarled Asher. "This is no place for a boy. Or a girl."

The words were meant to sting, but they rang true to Dov's ears. Just then there was no doubt what he needed to do. He grabbed Kiva's hand and headed for the way out.

"Come on." He tried not to sound as gruff as Asher, Menahem, and the others. "I'll get you out of here."

And Dov didn't just mean the dark hideout. Forget Natan and his friends. Forget the greasy rifle lying in the rubble. Forget everything. For once, he knew exactly what to do next. He just didn't quite know *how* to do it.

At least not yet. That would come.

"Where are we going?" Kiva asked, stumbling along beside him.

"They were right." He didn't have time for questions and answers.

"They were?"

"You don't belong here, so I'm getting you out of here. If it's the last thing I do, I'm going to get you and your friends out of the Old City."

That was easier to say than to do, of course. Back at the apartment, Mrs. Elazar and Mrs. Lieberman were trying to feed a dozen orphans and the three Elazar girls with a meal for two. No one complained, but Dov's own stomach rumbled in protest.

"I'm sorry, children." Mrs. Elazar ladled the thin soup into their cups. A tiny dumpling floated on the shimmering surface of Kiva's cup. "This is the best we can do today. Perhaps tomorrow another convoy will make it through with supplies."

Perhaps.

Out in the crowded living room, Reb Herschel's glasses lay carefully folded over his copy of the Scriptures. Dov scanned the open page, looking for answers in a story full of spies, hiding, and battles with Hittites, Hivites, Perizzites, Girgashites, Amorites, and Jebusites. The book of Joshua.

Dov smiled at the strange names. This would be the story of Jericho, where the walls came tumbling down. Dov didn't know too many stories from the Scriptures, but he had heard this one. He slid the glasses aside before picking up the text, and he read for himself about Joshua and the spies scouting out the enemy city of Jericho.

"I pray . . . you will save alive my father"—Dov read what Rahab had said to the Jewish spies—*"and my mother, and my brethren . . . and deliver our lives from death."*

Dov wondered what it would have been like to have his father saved from death, and his mother, too. *It happened for Joshua, didn't it?*

Only not for him.

Rahab, on the other hand—she was the one trapped in a city surrounded on all sides by enemies. Maybe she had a lot in common with Joshua, who had to do his own escaping before the battle. Maybe she had something in common with Dov, too. He couldn't help reading on to see what happened.

"Then she let them down by a cord through the window; for her house was upon the side of the wall. . . ."

He stared at the words for a long moment as if they were a message from God just for him. A rope over the wall?

Could that work? Maybe. But he knew he couldn't do it alone. Who could help him?

Without another word Dov marched to a corner of the tiny kitchen, pulled his transmitter from the shelf, and stretched out the wire antenna. He looked at the clock. Almost six in the evening.

If everything was on schedule, Emily's uncle Anthony and aunt Rachel would be setting up their own radio equipment for broadcast. Would they hear him? He tapped the battery. If it worked, perhaps someone listening would hear and give them his message.

I'll probably have only one chance.

If he was lucky, Dov thought he'd be able to send one more message to his Haganah friends on the other side of the wall. And if things went the way he hoped, that would be all he'd need to tell them what he was planning for the twelve orphan girls. Just like Rahab and Joshua, he'd "let them down by a cord."

If it was good enough for Joshua, it's good enough for a bunch of orphans like them. Like us.

Dov glanced out through the kitchen window at the growing moon. In a few days the night would be almost as bright as day.

Moon or no moon, in a few days they would make their escape over the wall.

Just like Joshua.

MARGOA

10

For the next hour Emily trudged up and down in the mud between metal huts. Over and over she asked the same question.

"Do you know Leah Zalinski of Warsaw?"

Many of the people she asked only stared right through her. Even when they answered, it was always the same: "No Leah Zalinski here."

"No worries, miss." Nick had caught up with her after unloading his potatoes. "Names change. Sometimes different."

Emily thought about that, trying to decide if it was good news or bad. She remembered reading that Dov's brother, Natan, had changed his name from Zalinski to Israeli. But she doubted the boys' mother would do the same. Wouldn't she want her sons to be able to find her?

"We go now?" Nick asked her. "Come back again, if you want."

Emily looked at the crowd of boys and girls following them through the teeming camp. They all wore castoffs from who knows where. Rags, really. They'd trailed along behind her as if it were a sport. Now the youngest ones looked up at her with sad saucers for eyes, as if they expected another potato or handout.

"I'm sorry," she told them. But she couldn't look straight into their sad, dark eyes, just as she couldn't look straight into the searing Mediterranean sun. If she hadn't done anything wrong, why did she feel so guilty?

"I really am sorry," she repeated. Still, the sight of these little ones reminded her of a Bible verse she'd once learned in Sunday school. Only, it had never before hit her so painfully.

"Inasmuch as ye have done it unto one of the least of these my brethren, ye have done it unto me."

If that were true . . . Emily hadn't done much to help anyone yet. Emily kept walking, trying to ignore the mud that caked the soles of her shoes, making them heavier with each step. She tried not to think of how much her feet had started to ache.

"Just one more row," she mumbled and marched up to the next door.

But she never had to knock; the children announced their coming clearly enough. This time an old man in baggy, wrinkled castoffs came to the door, and he listened patiently to her questions. His eyebrows shot up at the mention of the name.

"You know the name?" she asked, taking the clue. "Zalinski?"

The man rattled off a string of Polish in response, holding out his hand as if he expected an answer.

"Does anyone know what he just said to me?" Emily looked around the small crowd, but no one volunteered to translate.

Dear! Emily wondered what to do next. *Finally someone who can help, but he can't understand me—nor I him.*

"Margoa," said the man, waving. "Margoa."

"Margoa," she repeated. "What is Margoa?"

Or who? She knew the word was Hebrew for *rest*. But that made no sense. Again she turned to the small crowd.

"Please, does anybody know what he means?" she asked them

in Hebrew. From a cluster of children, one was pushed to the front. He stood like a broomstick and toed the yellow mud with one worn leather shoe. Emily looked at his earnest face while his friends pulled back.

"Will you explain Margoa?" she asked him.

He nodded and turned to go.

"I don't know if he understood me," she called to Nick. "But I'm going to follow."

Her skinny helper sprinted through the mud, ignoring puddles and rain rivers. He skirted a group of olive-skinned refugees arguing over a tent that had collapsed in the rain.

This was probably not what poor Nick had in mind when he said he'd give an English girl a lift to the camps, she thought as Nick pounded along behind them.

Still, she followed to learn about this Margoa, their only real clue so far. Rest? Come to think of it, she could jolly well have used a rest. The boy was a pretty good runner. She'd heard most refugees were weak and feeble, still trying to recover their strength after the war. Not this one. Their young host hurdled over a sleeping dog and dodged between two tents near the far edge of the camp.

"Oh!" Emily felt her head jerk backward, and she slipped in the oozing mud.

A rope had caught her by the throat, and she gasped for breath. Nick vaulted over her just in time to avoid tumbling into two tents as they folded on top of her.

Natan tried to pace the room, but he couldn't get far, since the girls sat on the floor, right where he would have walked. Their heads silently followed every move. Dov watched his brother, too, and tried again to explain his plan.

"No. I just don't think it's a good idea." Natan clenched a fist behind his back. "It'll never work."

"Yes, it will. I can find some rope, and I'll find a basket they can sit in."

"A basket? That's crazy."

"It is not. It worked for Joshua."

"Oy!" Natan rolled his eyes. "Now you are telling us how Joshua did it. Next you'll be walking around with a staff like Moses, calling down manna from heaven."

"Oh, come on. You know we're running out of food. We have to get these girls out."

"All right. Suppose for a minute we did this crazy thing you're suggesting. What are you going to do, just drop them over the wall and—"

"No, no, no. Anthony and Rachel would be there. They can find a safe place for these kids if anybody can."

That was too much for Natan. "What are you talking about? Are you on some kind of mission or something? What's gotten into you?"

"What's gotten into *me*?" Dov counted as his temper burned. "Look, these girls are petrified, sick, starving . . . and people are shooting at them. How many more reasons do you need for getting them out of the Old City to someplace safer?"

"But you didn't even know these orphans *existed* until after you came to the Jewish Quarter. Why do you care so much all of a sudden?"

Dov paused for only a moment.

"I just know I'm supposed to do this, Natan. I *have* to do this."

"Did God order you to? I can just hear it now." Natan lowered his voice. " 'Dov Zalinski, my servant, thou shalt bring forth my children out of the Jewish Quarter of the Old City. Go forth, Dov!' Or is it Moses?"

"Stop it!" That was all Dov could take. "You can't talk to me like that!"

Dov spun toward his brother, grabbed him by the shirt collar with his left hand, and took a swipe with his right. Some of the younger girls screamed and scattered. Natan easily blocked the attack. But even if Dov had caught Natan off guard, the fight was over almost before it began. Mrs. Elazar was on both of them in an instant, grabbing them by their necks as if they were naughty puppies.

"You should be ashamed of yourselves!" she shouted. "I will not have God mocked, and I will not have fighting in this house. Out, both of you!"

She led them to the door as she continued her scolding.

"You two stay out there and cool off. Come back in with an apology—or not at all."

Natan straightened his shirt, took one cold look at his brother, and marched off toward the square.

"I've had it with you, Dov, you and your weird ideas! I think you're crazy in the head."

"I don't care what you think. I'm going to get those girls out of here."

"Suit yourself." Natan didn't look back. "You're on your own."

"Fine with me." Dov straightened his own shirt. Another button had come off, and the collar had ripped. "Go ahead and leave. See if I care!"

Dov crossed his arms and slid down with his back to the wall until he rested on a dusty doorstep. Too late to take back his words, he watched his brother stalk away.

What did I just do? He wiped a hot tear with his sleeve before anyone noticed. *Why did I have to get so mad?*

Natan stopped short when he reached the far end of the court-yard—almost as if he heard Dov's thoughts. He clenched and unclenched his fists but did not turn around.

"Dov?" Chava suddenly poked her head out the door. "Are you coming back in?"

Dov watched his brother slip around a corner.

"Why won't you just say you're sorry?"

He shrugged, but Chava wouldn't let it go.

"Mrs. Lieberman said—"

"Chava!" Mrs. Lieberman chided. "He'll come in when he's ready." She gave Dov a long look, eyebrows up, before pulling the young girl back inside. The thick door shut with a final *slam,* like a judge's gavel.

What now? Dov squinted up at the lead-colored clouds gathering above the Old City. They grew darker by the minute, matching his mood. Ten minutes went by, then twenty. Maybe longer.

This is crazy. He threw a small rock as hard as he could, bouncing it off a stone wall on the other side of the square. *But what did I expect—a word from God?*

Well, that might have been nice for once. He waited a few more minutes, but God didn't seem to be saying anything, even though Dov strained his ears. He couldn't make out God's voice in the thunderclouds drifting up from the west. A stray drop of rain splattered on Dov's nose.

Why can't I hear you? Dov wondered.

God's voice certainly wasn't in the sound of shooting that started a few minutes later. The clatter of gunshots echoed through the courtyard, enough to make Dov melt back into the doorway for shelter. The echoes made it hard to know where the shots were coming from.

Little Chava's nose peeked out the door once again.

"Dov!" she whispered.

Was that the voice he had been waiting for? That of a squeaky seven-year-old girl with a ponytail?

Dov wasn't sure, but he still knew what he had to do, even if he had to do it alone. And he couldn't do it by standing out there in the street.

"Dov?" The whisper came louder this time. "You have to come back in!"

"I'm coming." He finally turned to go back inside. "I need to tell you something very important. You and your friends."

GRAVESTONE CLUE

A moment after the collision, Emily and Nick found themselves surrounded by at least a dozen surprised people. Who would dare trip over their tent homes?

"I'm terribly sorry." Emily held out her muddy hands after Nick helped her up. "I didn't see the rope. We'll help you put up your tents again."

An older woman frowned and stared at her. For that matter, no one else looked very happy with Emily's apology, either. Not that she blamed them. Emily felt the stinging rope burn on her neck and guessed it was probably turning into a serious welt.

"We were just looking for Margoa," she explained. "Do you know it?"

If they did, they weren't saying. And when Emily looked from one person to the next, she thought she had a better feeling for what it might be like to have leprosy.

"What's wrong?" she whispered to Nick, who shook his head. "Why do they just ignore me?"

A couple of young men began grimly setting up the tent without another word. Whatever Margoa meant, it did not bring smiles to the faces of these people.

"We should go," Nick told her, pointing to their young helper. The boy had come back for them; he peeked around the corner of another tent and waved for them to follow.

"So sorry," Emily repeated as she tried to wipe the mud off her hands and arms. At least she was wearing blue shipboard sailor's slacks and not a skirt. This time the people made way for her and Nick, and they caught up with the boy, away from the tents.

"Margoa," he told them, pointing to an open area at the far corner of the camp, far from any tents or huts, past a row of foul-smelling latrines.

Emily squinted, still not understanding. She put her hand on the boy's shoulder, but he pulled away.

"Show me," she asked, knowing he would not understand. Instead, he took one more look at the lonely corner and ran back toward the maze of tents. He had obviously decided his job was done.

"Is this Margoa?" Emily took a few careful steps closer. And then a knee-high stone with a small inscription caught her attention.

Margoa Cemetery.

Of course. There was no mistake. As tradition allowed, each gravestone in the small cemetery was carefully chiseled in Hebrew letters. And after growing up in Jerusalem, Emily needed no interpreter to make out the names.

Leo Catz (Born Leipsig, 1912. Died Famagusta, 1947). Miriam Yadin. Eliazar Sternberg. People who had almost made it to their Promised Land. Or perhaps they *had* made it, only to be turned back to this last insult, this last prison camp. Emily stumbled closer, folding her arms tightly, careful not to tread in the wrong places.

Here these people had come, and no further. Her tears mixed

with the drizzle until it became hard to read the names. *Ada Silberschmidt. Yaacov Reisman. Mishka Milstein.*

Mordecai Zalinski.

Emily caught her breath and stopped. So it was true. Dov's father's life really had been cut short before he could make it to Jerusalem to see the miracle of his son, Dov, still alive. Perhaps even Natan, too. Here, in a camp full of people who had lost entire families, was buried a man whose sons still lived.

Emily checked the date carved on Mordecai Zalinski's stone. *Born Warsaw, 1903. Died Famagusta, 1947.*

Her heart fell. If only she could have told him about Dov before it was too late! But Emily knew it was no use thinking that way. Now there was only one thing left to discover. Perhaps there was one more Zalinski in this graveyard. And if there was, she had to know. She had promised, after all.

But as they stood silently in the rain, Nick coughed quietly and glanced over his shoulder.

Emily looked, too.

They were not alone.

"There you are." Emily waved at their young guide, now only a hundred yards away. Maybe he could tell them more. Did anyone ever visit this grave? Did anyone know this man's wife?

But without a word the boy turned and hurried toward the edge of the nearest tent city.

"Wait!" Emily started to run. "I only want to ask you a question!"

The boy obviously had other ideas. And when Emily arrived at the tents a moment later, he was gone. Two girls watched her from the shelter of a small canvas canopy in front of one of the tents.

"Pardon me," she asked them, "but did you see a boy run through here just a moment ago?"

They shook their heads slowly and shrugged their shoulders.

"Does that mean no, or that you don't understand me?"

Silence.

"I see. Doesn't anyone speak Hebrew in this camp?"

Emily hurried on, peering into tents, then more huts. Everywhere she asked; everywhere she got the same answer.

"It's like before," she sighed. "No one knows anything."

And just when she thought she was lost again in the maze of muddy tents and tin huts, Nick hurried up behind her.

"I'm sorry, miss, but we have to go. I must make other deliveries, no?"

"Yes, of course. But just one more—I mean, I thought maybe . . . I don't know."

"Look, I come back again with more potato. You come, too?"

"When?"

He shrugged and held up his hands.

"Maybe tomorrow. Who knows? I wait for the British to call me. Come."

"Maybe tomorrow" turned into "maybe the next day." In the meantime, Emily saw little of Constance Pettibone, who was often found in the company of J.D. Roper in Famagusta. He had found his award-winning story, Emily supposed, and just had to finish writing it—if he ever took time off his lively social calendar, that is. In any case, soon he would return to New York, New York, and that would be the last of him.

Fine. Let him flirt with Constance and write his foolish story. Emily felt her own steam rising, like that of the tugs out in the harbor. And as the Friday morning sun peeked out from behind the clouds, she thought of the refugees waking up in their miserable, muddy tents, Dov's mother perhaps among them. But what could she do about it?

To make the time go faster, Emily spent that morning pacing the deck of the *Helgefjord,* watching birds in the harbor, waiting, and praying. Or perhaps she was just complaining to God. Sometimes she wasn't quite sure she knew the difference.

God *had* brought her to Cyprus for a reason, hadn't He?

She waited for an answer but heard nothing. No voices from heaven, no thundering "Yes!" or "Do this!"

"Maybe not," she sighed, doubting her earlier certainty. But by eleven-thirty Emily decided she could at least try to call Nick Papakostas from a lobby telephone at the Savoy Hotel. After all, it was Friday. Soon it would be a week since they'd arrived in Cyprus.

"So sorry, Miss Emily," Nick told her over the crackly connection a short time later. No matter that it was probably just across town. "No today. Tomorrow, perhaps. I let you know."

"Oh." Emily couldn't hide the disappointment from her voice. "You're sure?"

"But not to worry, eh? Good news. I talk to my priest about finding your friend's mother."

"You mean—" Emily wasn't sure if that meant he had already talked to his priest, or that he was going to.

"Father Athenasios says you will not find her."

"Pardon?" This was good news?

"He says that if she lives, she will find *you.*"

"And how precisely will she do *that*?" Emily snapped—then instantly regretted her sharp tongue. But honestly, how would he know such a thing?

"I'm sorry, Miss Emily. I only tell you what he tells me."

Emily swallowed hard and tried to fight back the tears. She should never have gotten involved in this mess.

"No, I'm the one who's sorry. Please thank your Father Athen—"

"Athenasios."

"Yes, you will thank him for me, won't you?"

"Sure, Miss Emily. Maybe I see you tomorrow. But you will promise not to go alone, eh?"

Emily sighed. Nick had turned out to be more of a protector than she'd first thought. Perhaps that wasn't all bad.

"I'll wait."

Emily hung up the phone gently, wiped her eyes with the corner of her embroidered handkerchief, and did her best to escape the lobby without seeing anyone she knew from the ship. She tried not to think about what Nick had told her as she wandered the dusty, narrow streets of Famagusta.

More waiting? Naturally. She turned the corner, choosing the long way back to the *Helgefjord.* But she didn't notice the loose cobblestone. . . .

"Ow!" Emily stubbed her sandaled toe, hop-scotched a few steps, and did her best to stay clear of an oncoming taxi. The wheezing car's driver gave her a toothless smile, perhaps hoping she might hire him.

Not this time. Instead she hurried along, keeping an eye out for more loose stones. And she steered safely clear of the alley with the unfriendly pack of dogs. She hadn't yet made it back to the pier, though, when a familiar horn greeted her from behind.

"Oh!" Emily jumped for her life and peeked back over her shoulder.

"Miss Emily, is good news!" Nick Papakostas hung out the side of his truck and slapped the door. He might have paved her into the cobblestones if she hadn't hopped out of the way quickly enough.

Good news? she wondered. *I hope not more from Father Athenasios!*

She bit her lip for thinking such a rude thing but managed to be pleased she hadn't said it.

"You never believe. I hang up phone, talking to you. Almost same time"—he snapped his fingers—"is call from English captain. He says, 'Pick up Jewish fish at the pier.' I say, 'How soon?' and he tells me, 'Right now!'"

"Right now?" Emily guessed it was just after noon. A late start, if they were to make it to the camp today.

"So do you come?"

"I have to tell Miss Pettibone."

"Sure. I load the truck. You tell your Miss Pettyphone."

"That would be Miss Pettibone."

"Is what I said, too."

Emily smiled for the first time all day and ran for the ship. Perhaps Nick's priest was right about finding—or not finding— Leah Zalinski. And perhaps God had finally spoken to her through this. What else could Emily do but follow along?

"What is the fish for?" she asked less than an hour later. The back end of Nick's truck was piled high with wooden crates—all of them leaking melted ice water and smelling rather fishy.

"I was thinking you should know," Nick told her as they hurtled up the hilly road. This time he didn't play the part of the tour guide, only the race car driver. "Is carp from Palestine. Special delivery! Hurry before sundown, they tell me, before Sabbath sundown. I hear there is special Jewish festival tonight in the camp. You tell Miss Pettibone?"

Emily nodded. "I left a note. She was out again with that—"

"Pushy American newspaper man!" He finished her sentence, and they both laughed. "They should come to festival instead."

Festival? For a moment Emily searched her memory. April, springtime in Jerusalem . . . of course! "That would be *Pesach*. A little late this year, but—"

Her mind drifted back to the times she had celebrated with their Jewish friends in Jerusalem. This was her favorite feast, full of symbols and reminders of the Messiah. The wine, the unleavened bread, so much more . . .

"Pesach?" Nick sounded as if he had never heard of such a thing.

"The Passover holiday. It has other Hebrew names, as well."

Like *Hag ha-Matzot*, Feast of the Unleavened Bread, from the Bible book of Exodus. *Hag ha-Pesah*, from when God's Angel of Death "passed over" the homes of the Hebrew slaves in Egypt, those who were protected by the sign of the lamb's blood on their doorframes. Or *Z'man Herutenu*—season of our freedom, the rabbis said.

But if this is a season of freedom, Emily thought, *then what a very odd celebration for Jews in a dreary detention camp.*

Or perhaps this was more like that first Passover than anyone realized.

"Your pass, Miss Emily?" Nick's words interrupted her thoughts as they reached the gate of Camp 70 with their load of carp on ice. "You show the pass they gave you last time."

She quickly fished the wrinkled yellow pass from her pocket and prayed that Nick's Father Athenasios might be right.

This time she left Nick outside the dining hall and hurried straight toward Margoa Cemetery. And though she shivered at the thought of seeing the bleak gravestones again, it was the only place to begin her search.

But something was different in the camp that afternoon. From one Quonset she heard a girl singing, from another, a lovely violin solo: a sad, lilting song Emily had never heard before. And everywhere, people cleaned and scrubbed. One woman sweeping the dirt floor of her tent actually looked up and smiled.

"Hag Sameach!" she called out as Emily hurried past. "Happy holiday!"

Perhaps it was.

Emily's heart leaped when she came to Mordecai Zalinski's gravestone.

Rocks! Someone had placed a handful of small gray stones on top of the marker. Like flowers, it was the Jewish way of honoring the memory of a loved one.

But who put them there?

PASSOVER
SURPRISE

Emily stood quietly in the gathering shadows past the edge of Margoa Cemetery, listening to the tent people getting ready for their Friday Pesach celebration. Minutes turned to an hour, and gray shadows around the stone markers slowly stretched into darkness. And still no one had come to visit the grave of Mordecai Zalinski.

Of course not, Emily scolded herself in her hiding place behind a patched army tent. She tried to unfold her legs from crouching so long. *Why would anyone show up just because I'm waiting here?*

She knew by this time Nick had to be wondering what was taking her so long; or perhaps he would leave without her. But still Emily could not leave her place. She hunched silently and watched dim lights come on in the camp like fallen stars. In the tents around and behind her, people began lighting lanterns and candles, one by one. Emily drank in the eerie blue light of the full moon, the fresh breeze coming off the ocean, the soft sound of singing.

As the sun set, a deep tenor began to hum in the tent nearest Emily, and she could not resist slipping quietly to a place where she could watch the drama.

"Dayenu . . ." The haunting melody floated through the camp. Dayenu, the song of God's blessings.

"Dayenu," repeated the song. *It is enough.*

Through a slit in this tent, Emily could just see a family gathered around a low table—actually, a board covered by a blue cloth. In the middle, a stump of candle planted in a small bucket of sand lit up the Passover feast of wine, unleavened *matzah* bread, bitter herbs, a hard-boiled egg, fish, and a tin that probably held the traditional salt water.

Even here, they had enough. Dayenu.

At the head of the table a husky, broad-shouldered man with a grizzled face leaned back on his side, his hat pulled over the back of his head. To his right sat a boy with hollow cheeks, younger than Emily. He wore a white *yarmulke*, the Jewish skullcap. And to the man's left sat his wife, her eyes shining brightly and a trembling smile on her thin lips.

At the father's words his wife rose to light a celebration candle—only a stub, really, but still a candle.

"Baruch ata Adonai," her voice quavered a bit as she spoke the Hebrew blessing, *"Elohaynu melek ha-olam . . ."*

"Blessed art Thou, O Lord our God, King of the Universe. . . ."

The father looked around at them with a smile of his own and hardly glanced at his tattered *Haggadah* service book before breaking into another song.

This was the Passover—a time for remembering the story of how a mighty God had brought His people out of Egypt and slavery to freedom. For these people, Emily knew, it was more than a story: The same God who had rescued the Hebrews from Pharaoh had now brought them out of slavery under the Nazis.

But what had He brought them to? More of the same?

"Mah nishtanah ha-laila hazzeh mikol ha-leilot?" read the young

son in lispy Hebrew. "Why is this night different from all other nights?"

By tradition, that would be the first of the four questions he would ask from the Haggadah book. Now the question rang true in Emily's ears, as if she could have asked it herself.

Yes, something *was* special about this night.

"Our people were slaves in Egypt for four hundred years before they were allowed to come home," the father told his family. "And now here we sit on *Erev Yisrael,* the Eve of Israel. Just as the day before the Sabbath is Erev Shabbat, for us this island is the erev before the promise. Tonight we celebrate our freedom to come."

Freedom to come, not freedom present.

For a moment Emily forgot about the grave, about her search for Leah Zalinski. Instead she stood frozen like a moth, staring at the light of the candle and listening. More than anything just then, she wanted to fly into the warmth and the light. She shivered in the cool breeze but did her best not to make a sound. That did not keep her from being discovered.

"You came to celebrate with us?" asked a soft voice. "I was told we had an English visitor."

Emily's heart nearly stopped at the question.

Dov peeked out the window to see if Natan might show up after all. But no. He hadn't been by all day. Evening had fallen in the Jewish Quarter—a Sabbath evening, no less—and it was painfully obvious that Natan would not be sharing the Pesach meal with them.

"We should start." Reb Herschel cleared his throat and looked toward Dov. "Would you like to follow along with me?"

Dov looked down at the lines in Reb Herschel's Haggadah

book. As the youngest boy in a room packed full of girls, it had fallen on him to play the part of the questioner. Mr. Lieberman had even found him a dusty yarmulke to wear as his wife brought out the food. Had their son once worn it? And as Mrs. Lieberman—the woman of the house—lit her candles and said the first blessing, each of the young scrubbed faces glowed in the flickering golden light.

"So we will use our imaginations a bit more this year." Mrs. Lieberman smiled an apology. There would be real matzah bread, about as hard as one-hundred-year-old shoe leather and only enough for a mouse-sized nibble, but real enough. Somehow she'd found an egg, too, and boiled it. Dov thought it looked more like a pigeon egg than a real chicken egg. Perhaps it was the last egg in the Jewish Quarter. He was looking forward to seeing how it could be divided twenty ways, as well.

"We even have fish!" clucked Mrs. Lieberman. She beamed as she opened a battered can of pickled herring. "So it's not exactly fresh, but who's checking?"

It didn't seem to matter to anyone else, either.

"And did we pick enough bitter herbs?" asked Golda.

Dov covered his smile. If there was one thing they had plenty of, it was bitter herbs. Under Reb Herschel's watchful eye, the girls had fanned out across the courtyard that afternoon, searching for dandelion leaves. It had become a race to see who could pick the most in the fastest time. And by the looks on their faces when they tasted the washed greens, they'd done just fine at finding something bitter. In a few minutes they'd succeeded in picking a heaping bowl full of leaves. That would be quite enough, Reb Herschel told them with a smudge of a grin on his face.

After several blessings and the first cup of thanksgiving, finally it was Dov's turn. He looked out the window for his brother one last time, took a breath, and delivered his line.

"Why is this night different from all other nights?"

"Our people were slaves in Egypt for many years," Reb Herschel responded. They all knew the story. Even the youngest orphans must have heard it, though they listened as if for the first time. "And tonight we celebrate our freedom from slavery. Tonight we celebrate our freedom to come."

As Reb Herschel went on, Dov almost forgot where he was. And he almost believed the words about freedom as he stared at the dim, flickering candle. Almost . . . until the dull *thump* of nightly explosions and the crack of gunfire rattled the low table Mrs. Lieberman had set.

Emily spun to face a small woman, probably younger than she looked. This was a survivor, after all, and most survivors in this camp looked worn and tired. Years of pain had bent this woman's shoulders—as if she had been carrying far too much weight, far too many miles. Deep lines left trails on her face like dark canyons. But the resemblance made Emily gasp in shock.

In those dark, sparkling eyes, Emily saw her friend. . . .

"Dov," she whispered, then clapped her hand over her mouth. Was it really?

The woman looked at her curiously, then leaned forward as if to take in Emily's scent, like one animal meeting another for the first time.

"I'm sorry, I didn't quite hear you." The woman's English sounded as perfect as Emily's, with a musical touch of northern England, perhaps the Lake District. Dov had mentioned his mother had been raised in Britain. But the accent sounded so oddly out of place in that camp that it startled Emily all over again.

It can't be, Emily told herself, all the while knowing it could—

it *had* to be. No one else could look more like her son than this mother. There was no mistaking.

"Pardon me for staring." But Emily couldn't have unglued her steady gaze if she'd wanted to. "It's just that you look so much like . . . your son."

At that the curious light in the woman's eyes clouded over, and she frowned and turned away. From inside the tent the father broke into song once more.

"You are mistaken." The woman's voice had turned flat, life-less. "I have no son. No husband. No family."

"But—" Emily caught her breath in a moment of doubt. Perhaps her hope had clouded her vision and she had only seen what she had hoped so badly to see. Perhaps it was a cruel trick her mind had played on her.

Was this woman really alone, the way she said?

When their eyes met again, Emily knew better. Instantly, though, she regretted the stab of pain she had caused—even with the truth—and she reached out to touch the woman's shoulder.

"Mrs. Zalinski? Mrs. Zalinski, please tell me it's you. You have to be—you look so much like him. And I promised Dov that I'd find you, and now God brought me to this island, and . . ."

The woman looked up to face Emily, only inches away, almost nose to nose. The flickering golden light from inside the nearby tent played shadows across her face. Emily almost flinched at the darker scowl, the pinched eyes. Even so, the look held a touch of confusion and a spark of hope.

Emily tried once more. "Please, Mrs. Zalinski. You must believe me. Dov is alive."

At that the woman wobbled on her feet, and Emily reached out to steady her. Emily wasn't sure she could keep her from falling, but she would try.

"No." The woman shook her head. "It cannot be true."

"It is true. I saw him just over a week ago." Emily could barely manage the words. "In Jerusalem."

The woman laughed in disbelief. " 'Next year in Jerusalem'? We always said we would go there someday. If you are lying, it is a wonderful lie you tell. But—how else could you know his name?"

Tears trickled down Mrs. Zalinski's cheeks, like the rain in the camp valleys, as she reached out to feel Emily's cheek, damp with her own tears.

"I saw . . . your husband's grave." Emily looked over the woman's shoulder in the direction of Margoa Cemetery. "I am so sorry."

They stared at each other for an agonizing moment. Again Emily was struck by the eyes, so much like Dov's.

And finally Leah Zalinski took a deep breath to reply.

"For these long years I have prayed for my sons every day, every hour. I have hoped with everything I was. But then I gave them to God, as I gave up my husband. Alone, I had given up hope. And now when you say these things, these dreams, they hit me in the heart."

"It's not a fantasy. It's real."

This time Mrs. Zalinski seemed to hear Emily, or at least she nodded in polite agreement. Now they both stared at the cemetery markers.

Emily had to know. "Can you tell me, if you don't mind my asking . . . about Dov's father? When did—"

"He died a month before I arrived at this place." Mrs. Zalinski followed Emily's gaze. "I had not seen him since 1942, when the Nazis arrested him.

"He was so handsome. With his fine dark hair and his broad shoulders. And that laugh of his. He made everyone around him smile. And such a strong man, too, only . . . not quite strong enough."

"I . . . I'm so sorry." Emily felt another stab of pain, deeper this time. It nearly took her breath away, as if she had lost someone from her own family. She might never hear all the stories—who was she to ask? But right now she could share the tears.

Mrs. Zalinski turned away and coughed, holding a handkerchief to her mouth and nose. The deep, rattling wheeze would not stop but seemed to suck all the breath out of the frail woman, and then some.

"Are you all right?" Emily put her arm around Mrs. Zalinski's shoulder, but the woman only turned her face away to gasp and wheeze once more.

"Yes, yes. I'm getting better."

"Pardon me for saying so, but if this is better, I would hate to have heard worse."

Mrs. Zalinski quickly but carefully folded her handkerchief and replaced it in a skirt pocket.

"Oh dear." Mrs. Zalinski shook her head as if to clear the cobwebs. "Whatever has become of my manners? You must forgive me."

"Not at all. You have nothing for which you should apologize."

But Mrs. Zalinski stood up straight and held out her hand. "Once upon a time we used to introduce ourselves, before such things as manners and dignity were taken from us. I am Leah Zalinski, and I am very pleased to meet you, Miss. . . ?"

Emily took the outstretched hand and held on tightly with both of her own.

"Emily. Emily Jane Parkinson. I am very pleased, as well. You don't know what this means to me."

"People told me an English girl was looking for me." Mrs. Zalinski smiled, and it seemed to light up the space between them like a Passover candle. "But they didn't mention she was such a *pretty* English girl. Or that she had such wonderful news."

And then the questions followed, slowly at first, but soon as if in a happy waterfall: Was Dov well? What was he like? Had he grown into a tall boy, like his father? Did he know she was alive? What about Natan, Dov's older brother? Was there any word of Natan?

Emily did her best to tell what she knew, beginning with the time she helped Dov on the beach after his refugee ship was captured by the British and they were both pushed over the railing into the sea. As Mrs. Zalinski hung on every word, Emily explained how they both swam to shore in the confusion of the soldiers shooting into the water. But she stopped in mid-sentence, stung by her own words.

"Something just occurred to me," said Emily.

Mrs. Zalinski's eyebrows lifted ever so slightly.

"If Dov had been captured back on that beach, instead of escaping with me, *he* would be here, not me. You would have been meeting your son instead of me."

Mrs. Zalinski only waved her hand. "You can't think like that, child. What happened, happened. It does no good to wonder what might have been or . . ."

But she didn't finish her sentence. Instead she collapsed into another fit of coughing, falling to her knees as she did.

"Mrs. Zalinski!" cried Emily.

FINAL PAGE

13

"Oh dear." Mrs. Zalinski's eyelids fluttered when she looked up at the small crowd gathered by a cot in a dim corner of the tent. "I must have fainted for a moment."

"We were worried about you." Emily sat on the foot of the bed. The family that had moments before been celebrating their Pesach meal crowded around for a better look.

"You will stay still," commanded the broad-shouldered father. "My daughter ran to fetch the doctor."

"I'm sure he's gone home for the night. It's Passover, after all." Mrs. Zalinski tried to swing her feet out of the cot, but Emily pushed them back.

"Please don't get up. You really need a doctor."

"It's just a cough." But her weak voice sounded less than convincing. "Please, it's the *children* who need the doctor. Not me."

"Perhaps so. But you do, too."

"I would not want to take any of his time as long as there are sick children in this camp." Mrs. Zalinski coughed into her pillow.

She coughed again, and Emily patted her on the back. What else could she do?

"So, what seems to be the trouble here?"

Everyone turned to see a ruddy, fresh-faced young man of no more than twenty-five years standing at the door of the family's tent with a small black bag in his hand.

"*You're* the doctor?" Emily hadn't meant it to sound the way it did. He ignored her comment and brushed into the tent. The two kids retreated to a safe distance, but Emily wouldn't leave the bed. Now that she had finally found Dov's mother, she wasn't about to let her out of her sight. Especially not with the young . . .

"Leftenant Hugh Daniels," he announced, dropping his open black bag directly on top of a plate of ceremonial matzah bread. "And who are—"

"Papa!" gasped the young boy, pointing with his eyes at the bag. "Look what he did!"

But the father warned his son into silence with a shake of his head, then closed his eyes and moved his lips, as if praying. Leftenant Daniels seemed not to notice his error, only squinted curiously at Emily. Perhaps she looked more out of place than she'd realized.

"It's just that . . ." she began. "Well, we were expecting someone, er . . ."

"Someone older, of course," snapped the leftenant, whose rank in the British army equaled that of *lieu*-tenant. "But at this time of the night, a field medic like me is the best you can hope for. Of course, if you'd rather I returned to my dinner, I'd be quite happy to oblige."

"Oh no. It's not that. We're all quite thankful you stopped by."

"Not all of us," whispered Dov's mother before launching into yet another coughing fit. "I certainly don't need a doctor—or a field medic—to tell me I have a bit of a cough. You should be off tending to the children."

And though she again carefully covered her mouth with her

handkerchief, this time even Emily could see it was more than "a bit of a cough."

"Oh my." The medic covered his nose and mouth and took a half step back as Dov's mother looked with wide eyes at the telltale red stain in her handkerchief.

"Oh dear," she whispered.

"Indeed." Daniels nodded. Perhaps he was more used to treating battle wounds and brave soldiers, but he obviously knew enough to recognize the sure signs of tuberculosis, the deadly lung disease. "I shan't need to examine you further, Mrs. . . . er . . ."

"Her name is Zalinski," said Emily, not sure how to help. "Leah Zalinski. And there *is* something you can do for her, is there not?"

"We'll see." The leftenant snapped his bag shut. "Of course, there are no guarantees, especially with an advanced case of tuberculosis such as this."

"How do you know how advanced it is?" Emily felt her cheeks warming, her face turning fire red. "You haven't even *looked* at her yet!"

But the leftenant was already on his way out. In his panic he stumbled over a pair of worn shoes by the tent flap.

"Make sure she rests in bed," he told them from behind the hand covering his mouth. His face looked as ashen as the pale evening light. "I'll see about getting her a bottle of cod liver oil."

"But a doctor?" Emily followed him outside. "What about a real doctor?"

He shook his head. "That's all I can do at the present. A *real* doctor, as you say, could not offer you more hope than I. There's really nothing else to be done, although I would advise you to keep a distance from this patient."

Emily felt as if she could beat this cowardly leftenant with her fists.

"Surely that's not *all* you can do." She grabbed the handle of his bag, forcing him to spin around.

"If you please, Miss—" He pulled his bag away.

"Parkinson." Emily might have drilled holes through the leftenant with her stare. "Emily Parkinson. My father is Major Alan Parkinson. And this *patient,* as you call her, sir, is a friend of our family."

The announcement hit him like a slap. Emily could almost hear the grinding of gears in the young man's head. After all, majors outranked leftenants by a good measure.

The hint of an embarrassed smile played at his lips as he cleared his throat. "I had no idea, Miss, er, Parkinson." Daniels' eyes had grown larger than before. "As I said, I'll look into securing your friend a bed at the military hospital in Nicosia."

"How soon?" Emily hated to use her father's name the way she just had. But how else could she get the young medic's attention?

"Immediately. We'll inform you as soon as a transport is available. Perhaps in a day or two."

She nodded as the man hurried off. At least he had bothered to come.

"Do you want me to read you more about what the American doctor says about treating tuberculosis?" Emily looked up from the dog-eared copy of *The Modern Home Medical Adviser* edited by Morris Fishbein, M.D. Half the pages were missing, but the book was in better condition than many of the castoffs lining the shelves of Camp 70's makeshift library.

"You could read me anything you like," answered Dov's mother. She lay still in her cot, her eyes closed. "I enjoy listening to your sweet voice, dear. This past day of knowing you and having you visit with me has been quite a treat, though you shouldn't have come."

"Of course I should have." Emily looked around the bare little tent from her perch on a hard wooden stool. She'd set up everything as Dr. Fishbein had directed in his book: the cot, the clean linen, even the paper sack for used handkerchiefs. She wasn't sure what the doctor would have said about the hard-packed dirt floor, but what could she do about that? She found her place on page 333 in the "Tuberculosis" section and started reading.

" 'The patient with tuberculosis who becomes discouraged, hopeless, pessimistic, or rebellious—' "

"That would be me."

" '—is difficult to treat and aids in his downfall. When a person first learns that he has this disease, he is likely to be upset and depressed. Knowing nothing of modern care, he is likely to feel that the disease will be promptly' . . . er . . ."

"Go ahead and say it," Mrs. Zalinski said, as if she were reading over Emily's shoulder.

"Pardon me?"

" 'The disease will be promptly *fatal.*' Isn't that what it says?"

"Oh. Well . . ." Emily wished she had skipped over that sentence. She kept reading and underlined a passage with her finger. " 'However, the disease is curable if treated sufficiently early and sufficiently long.' "

"Sufficiently early . . ." echoed Mrs. Zalinski. They both knew that was not the case with her. No one needed to say it. Leah Zalinski appeared to be in the final stages of a deadly disease.

"And it says here—"

"Please excuse me for interrupting, dear"—Mrs. Zalinski held up her hand—"because I'm certain I've mentioned this already. But do you really think you should be spending so much time with a sick person like me?"

"Oh." Emily thought for only a moment. "Well, we're doing just what Dr. Fishbein says in the book. I'm being quite careful."

"Hmm. Perhaps you'll be a doctor someday, too."

Emily grinned at the idea. "And besides, they're going to take you to the hospital in Nicosia in the morning. You're going to be all right."

"If God is willing." Mrs. Zalinski shifted again in her cot. "But let's not talk about my aches and pains anymore. Tell me again how you found Dov."

And so Emily told the story once more while Dov's mother closed her eyes and nodded. She seemed to hold to every word like a treasure. Afterward, Mrs. Zalinski even let slip a few details of her own life during the war, how she found her way to the refugee camp, that sort of thing.

"But I'd much rather remember the good days in Warsaw, before the bad times." The woman's voice softened, and her face glowed with a gentle smile. "Back when we lived on Gensia Street, where I had a fine flower box hanging in front of the window that Mordecai built for me. He was always so handy. Natan and Dov would play in the street. . . ."

When the voice dropped to a whisper, Emily dropped to her knees and leaned closer to hear the rest of the story. Yet after a few minutes even the whisper was almost gone.

"It is good to remember," Mrs. Zalinski told Emily. "But now that my Dov has nearly grown up, I'm glad he has found such a good friend in you, Emily."

"I . . ." Even if Emily had something to say in reply, she would not have been able. She tried to clear her throat, when Mrs. Zalinski gripped her arm.

"If you ever see him again . . ." At that Mrs. Zalinski sank into another spasm of coughing, doing her best to cover her mouth.

"It's all right." Emily patted her new friend on the back. "You don't need to talk anymore."

But at last Mrs. Zalinski caught her breath enough to force out a few more words.

"No, please. If you ever see him again, I want you to pass along my love. And to tell him that his father and I are so very . . . proud of him."

"His father and I are proud of him," she said. Not *were.* Emily wondered if it was just a slip of the tongue, or if Leah Zalinski believed she was closer to joining her husband than anyone guessed. Here in this place of Erev Yisrael, the Eve of Israel, it seemed both cruel and fitting.

"Yes, of course, but—" Emily trembled to see Dov's mother fail so quickly, as if she was giving up now that she knew one of her sons was really alive. "You'll tell him yourself, won't you? You don't need me to do that for you. As soon as you recover enough to leave, I'm sure you'll be seeing him yourself."

"That would be nice." Her smile seemed far off, and her eyelids closed once more. "So nice."

"I asked a few people, and they seemed to think you may be in a group that could be discharged from the camp in a few weeks anyway. It's your turn."

But Mrs. Zalinski wasn't listening. With a sigh, she fell into a fitful sleep, and so began a wrestling match for each shallow breath. Her thin lips looked chapped and blue, but they tipped up at each end into a hard-fought smile . . . at what?

Emily wondered as she read on about experimental treatments for tuberculosis, about sun treatments, lung treatments, and how many thousands of people died from the disease each year. But then she could read no further; the last few pages had been torn out of the old book.

Lord Jesus, is this her final page? Emily prayed for the woman she had just met, this beautiful woman whom God had surely brought Emily into this camp to meet. She had no doubt. God had worked a miracle. Only, now that Emily had found Mrs. Zalinski, would God allow her to die? It didn't make sense. Emily's tears fell on a page showing a diagram of the heart, but she didn't much care until someone burst through the door.

"There you are!" announced J.D. Roper, out of breath. Emily quickly dried her tears on the sleeve of her dress and hoped he wouldn't notice. "I've been looking for you all over this infernal camp. You have no idea!"

"Shhh." She held a finger to her lips and pointed to Dov's mother.

"You can thank me later." He lowered his voice a notch. "But this is your lucky day."

ONE WAY OUT

14

Emily didn't think J.D. Roper's definition of a "lucky day" matched her own. For one thing, she didn't believe in "luck." Luck wasn't in the Bible, her father had always told her.

Still, the American had caught her attention.

"Hey, no need to thank me." He smiled and spread out his arms as if waiting for someone to give him a hug, though Emily kept a safe distance as they walked back to the camp gate to meet Nick. "I just had to call in a few favors to get two seats on this plane."

"I'm sure that's very nice of you, Mr. Roper, but—"

"I figured maybe I owed you one for the Pulitzer Prize I'm gonna win. You did get me into this dump with your 'my dad the major' line. Knowing you even helped get me in this time."

"It's not a *line,* as you call it."

"Whatever. But whaddaya think? Didn't you tell me yourself your daddy wanted you off this rock pronto?"

Emily found J.D.'s American slang terribly annoying at times. Whatever in the world did *pronto* mean?

"I shall have to cable him in Jerusalem first."

"Sure, you go ahead and do that. Just don't wait too long. Our puddle jumper takes off at sunup, and I aim to be on it."

Puddle jumper? Sunup?

"What about Miss Pettibone?" Emily wondered aloud. She was halfway surprised J.D. was offering Emily his precious second ticket, rather than his new girlfriend.

But the American only winked at Emily. "I had to think hard on that one, I'll grant you. Just between you and me, she's a real nice dame and all. It's just, ah . . . well, I'm not the type to get tied down, if you know what I mean."

Emily knew all too well what he meant. And for Miss Pettibone's sake, she was relieved he would be leaving so soon.

Back on the *Helgefjord* that evening, Miss Pettibone didn't seem so sure about Emily's new travel arrangements.

"Of *course* I think it's the right thing to do." Her face said otherwise, as if someone had done her a terrible wrong, like forgetting her birthday. "It's a splendid gesture, Jonathan. And it's only right that Emily should go with you to Rome. She can take a train and a ferry home to England from there."

"Hey, I'll take care of the kid. No charge. All the way to London if I have to." He slapped Emily on the back—too hard. Emily winced but said nothing. But she noticed a tear in Miss Pettibone's eye as they watched the harbor from their ship's deck. And Miss Pettibone still clutched the cable from Emily's father.

"Well, it's clear he wants you to go, isn't it?" Her voice broke over the sound of a gull's cry.

Emily had read it, too: *Do not delay any longer. Continue to Rome with Mr. Roper. British consul will meet you there.*

"I just feel lousy we couldn't get you a seat, too, Constance.

Terrible." The way J.D. told his sad story, he really *did* look disappointed—far more so than he had looked back in the camp, telling Emily about it. "But the plane is only a six-seater, and it's full up with diplomatic types and stuffed shirts. Believe me, I tried."

"I know, Jonathan. I know." The white handkerchief she used to dab at her eye was embroidered with the initials *JDR*. "But since it's my job to look after Emily's welfare . . ." Miss Pettibone took a deep breath. "I'll be glad to come later with her things."

Glad, thought Emily, as in *I really don't want to, but I must.*

"I'll write as soon as I get back to New York," J.D. told Miss Pettibone.

Emily almost glanced behind his back to see if he was crossing his fingers. *I'll bet you will.*

Considering the company, Emily wondered how she herself would survive a trip to Rome in J.D.'s "puddle jumper" plane. She wasn't looking forward to the time in his company. Even more, she wondered how soon Aunt Rachel and Uncle Anthony would get her cable about Mrs. Zalinski. Hopefully they could get word to Dov—soon.

"Look at her!" J.D. waved his hand at Emily. "Give a girl a way off Cyprus, and she looks as if we're ruining her day."

"It's not that." Emily stood her ground. "I simply thought I'd help out a bit more."

"Very noble of you, dear." Miss Pettibone patted Emily like a child, and it made Emily bite her bottom lip in anger. "Spending time at that wretched camp and all."

"It wasn't so noble."

"Well, whatever you call it, I wouldn't have let you go back if Jonathan hadn't promised to protect you. It was quite sweet of him, actually."

Sweet wasn't the word Emily would have used.

"So you've done what you could," offered J.D.

"Not yet." Emily shook her head. "You know I promised a friend back in Jerusalem I would try to find his mother, and—"

"And so you have," interrupted Miss Pettibone. "But those people are not your concern, and they are most certainly not *your* family."

"But it's almost as if she were my own mother!"

"Heavens, now you've rather crossed the line, don't you think? You make it sound as if this poor woman's life were in your hands."

"It's not." Emily knew better. "But she is my friend, and I can't leave her."

"Well, dear, I hope they've put your . . . *friend* in quarantine. I understand in these cases visitors are not allowed. It's for the best."

"Yeah, you don't mess with tuberculosis," added J.D. "And besides, I have a feeling your pop would want to hear about this."

Was that a threat? Let him tell her father!

"But don't worry, kid," he continued with his trademark smile. "We won't worry the old man unless we absolutely have to."

Emily wasn't sure what "unless we absolutely have to" meant. She would tell Father herself when she saw him again. Someday he would return to England, too, and she would tell him everything. But no matter how much these two said to discourage her, Emily couldn't escape the nagging feeling that she could do more to help Dov's mother. She *had* to.

If I don't, who else will?

Dear Dov . . . Emily's hand trembled as she added yet another piece of crumpled stationery to the growing pile at her feet, next to her packed bags. She glanced over at Miss Pettibone, still snoring in her bunk, wearing silly, black silk sleep blinders on her eyes.

Emily checked the alarm clock over her own bed.

Four o'clock. *Oh dear.*

Emily stifled a yawn as she quietly slipped a fresh sheet of paper from the drawer, wrinkled her forehead in thought, and started once more to spill out everything she could remember of what Mrs. Zalinski had told her the day before.

It only seems right that you should know what happened to your family, she began. *And you should know first of all that your mother is very sweet, very strong.*

Only not quite strong enough, she told herself, remembering how Mrs. Zalinski had said the same thing about Dov's father. But she could not bring herself to write those words.

So Emily told him what she had learned from Dov's mother about the war years. Even though the pain of hearing such memories felt raw and fresh, she told how Dov's family had survived after Mr. Zalinski was taken away. How Natan bravely went out to find food. What Mrs. Zalinski had done to live through the camps after being separated from Natan. Emily stopped for a moment to think how odd it seemed, writing this history for Dov, as if she had lived through it herself.

So many had *not* lived to tell their own stories; for now it was left to Emily to tell Dov his. So many had died during the war. Why had the Zalinskis survived? They'd worked hard to make it this far. She couldn't be sure, but it seemed Mr. Zalinski had been driven by the same desire as his sons. He had probably whispered the same words they had shouted just the day before yesterday in Camp 70 during the Passover celebrations:

"Next year in Jerusalem!"

Only, Dov's father hadn't quite made it to the city on the hill. And it hurt to think Dov's mother had no idea how her husband, Mordecai, had finally died—only that he had died alone. Now the disease that wasted at Leah Zalinski's lungs threatened to cut her down in the same place as her husband. Like Moses in the wilderness, the older Zalinski generation had made it only to the edge of the Promised Land, leaving it for their children to conquer.

She is so happy to know you are alive, Dov. And she didn't want you to be sad that she might not make it. She is just so happy, especially knowing that you might someday find your brother to lean on. . . .

"No." Emily sighed, crumpled the paper, and threw it into the pile with all the others. It wasn't right for her to tell this story. She would have to leave it to Dov's mother.

Just as he had for the past two days, Dov paced up the Street of the Steps, mapping out his escape. A yowling sound from beneath a pile of splintered wood made him jump.

"Who's that?" he said, then felt foolish that an alley cat could startle him so. At least no one else was there to see him, not at five in the morning.

I'm the only one crazy enough to be out here, he told himself. *Besides the cat, that is.*

At least it had quieted down. The nightly shooting from just over the towering Old City wall had ended for the night. Dov smiled to himself in the darkness before the dawn. He and the cat knew something no one else did.

"It's perfect, isn't it, fella?"

The cat obviously didn't care as it scurried off, so Dov climbed up over the rubble himself to look into the dark window of the bombed-out house. The family living there had left, probably weeks ago. And if he breathed wrong, it might collapse into a heap. But still it was perfect: The house wall leaned dangerously, perfectly close to the taller city wall. From the remains of its roof, it was only a short stretch to the stones atop the ancient, twelve-foot-wide Old City wall.

"Hey!" yelled a voice from behind and below him. "What are you doing up there, Dov?"

Dov fell sideways and into a crack between collapsed sections of the house. He grappled for balance but skinned his nose on a stone wall on his way down.

"Ooy!" he grunted and came to rest in a pile of rubble and dust. He turned in time to see Batya's round little face staring down at him.

"Are you okay?" Her tiny voice squeaked with concern. "I'm sorry! I didn't mean to scare you. I had to get up, and I saw you leave. I just wanted to see where you were going. Are you going to the outhouse, too?"

Dov tried to sit up in the rubble but only fell back again. She reached out her hand to help him, and he could not hold back a smile.

"No, Batya. I was just out for a little walk."

"But Reb Herschel said none of us should be out alone."

"That's right. We're not alone now, are we?"

Batya shook her head as Dov got to his feet and dusted himself off. But voices from the other side of the wall made him freeze. Batya must have heard them, too.

"Who is—"

Dov clamped a hand over her mouth before she could say another word. Without a sound they crouched in the rubble.

"Arab guards," he whispered into her ear. Just outside the gate.

So I wasn't the only one out for a walk, thought Dov.

"Please, Mrs. Zalinski." Emily tried to put up her hand. "I really think you should give that note to him yourself. It would mean so much more that way."

A nurse from the British Military Hospital leaned her head in the door. "Are you finished with your breakfast, Mrs. Zal—oh! I didn't realize you had a visitor."

"It's all right," Mrs. Zalinski said.

The starch-skirted nurse wasn't as sure. "Well, just another minute. Mrs. Zalinski needs to rest her first day here. I really shouldn't allow any visitors."

"Thank you." Emily nodded, then turned to Dov's mother and took the note. She glanced at the front of the envelope, where Mrs. Zalinski had carefully written: *To my son Dov.*

"You're a sweet girl to say I should give it to him myself." Mrs. Zalinski had closed her eyes again, as if she were far, far away. Her voice faded to the faintest whisper. "But you and I both know—"

"I already sent a cable to my aunt in Jerusalem," Emily interrupted her, even as she tried to put out of her mind what the grim-faced army doctor had told them. "I'm sure she'll be in touch with Dov to tell him about you."

"You've been so kind."

But it's not been enough! Emily wanted to shout. If only she could stay just a few more days. Even a few more hours. There was much more she wanted to say to this woman. So much more she wanted to know.

So much more.

"Miss?" The nurse tapped her white shoe on the gray tile floor—scrubbed and polished to a proper British shine.

Emily held up her hand. *One more minute!* The strong antiseptic smell made her want to sneeze, but it was surely better for Mrs. Zalinski here than in the refugee camp tent with its dirt floor.

"I wanted to stay." Her words seemed to fall flat. "But my father insists, you see."

"Of course he does." Mrs. Zalinski smiled weakly. "So do I."

Emily would have given her a big hug if the nurse hadn't still been hovering at the door, checking her wristwatch.

"Miss. Please. It's time."

"I'm coming." Emily stalled. "My aunt in Jerusalem, I'll try to contact her again—I *will* contact her, just as soon as I get back to England."

"You have my letter, Emily."

"Yes."

As Mrs. Zalinski broke into another coughing fit, the nurse finally pulled Emily into the hall.

"I'm afraid you *must* leave now, miss."

Emily waved back at her friend, and for a moment their eyes locked. She prayed her next words would be true.

"I'll see you again, Mrs. Zalinski. I don't know how, but I will. And I will pray for you."

Leah Zalinski's eyes smiled. She brought a limp hand up to wave before falling back into her pillow.

FLIGHT TO ROME

15

Two hours after Emily left the army hospital in Nicosia, she shaded her eyes from the assault of the bronze Cyprus sun and stepped onto the airport pavement. The sound of bells in the city behind her reminded Emily of how much she missed going to church every Sunday, back home in Jerusalem. Waves of late-morning heat shimmered all around her as she adjusted the handle of her flowered corduroy valise.

Everything I own, in this little suitcase. That was not quite so. Her father had arranged to ship other things in crates on the ship. But those would probably take several more weeks to follow her to England.

All the same, she felt like a homeless wanderer as she looked toward the airplane that would take her and three other passengers off the island.

"I'll be fine." Constance Pettibone patted the back of Emily's neck and gave her a quick, awkward hug. "Don't worry about me for a moment."

The thought of worrying about Miss Pettibone honestly hadn't crossed Emily's mind. She smiled and glanced over her shoulder at

J.D. Roper, and he blew a kiss in their direction—obviously intended for the cheek of Constance Pettibone. As their airplane revved its engines, he pointed at his wristwatch and motioned for Emily to hurry.

"I have to go." Emily raised her voice to announce the obvious. By that time Miss Pettibone's tears had reached full flood stage. She waved J.D.'s white handkerchief like a team flag as Emily scurried across the pavement and ducked behind the stormy wind from powerful twin propellers.

The plane itself hardly looked ready to fly, though Emily's hair flew quite well behind her in the propeller windstorm. She guessed from the pockmarks and charred paint on the side that this plane had seen the worst of the last war. Someone had tried to cover over the old British military markings on the wings and sides; perhaps they had run out of paint.

"Pretty nice, eh?"

Emily handed up her bag but pretended not to see J.D.'s outstretched hand reaching to her from inside the plane. A short length of fold-out boarding steps brought her into the six-seater plane.

"Well, it's the best I could manage," said the American, waving his hand around the padded passenger compartment. A bench seat lined the back wall, while two single seats were bolted right behind the pilot's and copilot's chairs.

"Hullo, am I the last one?" Emily took the single seat next to a bank of windows on the right side, while J.D. slid her valise behind the rear double seat. A thin-lipped older man in a gray suit and matching hair nodded politely but didn't introduce himself. Probably a diplomat or a businessman; he wouldn't be bothered in the backseat. He balanced a brown leather briefcase on his knees and studied a sheaf of papers.

"We're late. But I think we're still waiting on one more fella," reported the American. He waved again out the door at Miss Pettibone in the distance. "They told me we'd have a full load to Rome."

Sure enough, when Emily glanced out the window, she noticed a man in an ill-fitting suit push through the gate and hurry their direction. He looked vaguely Middle Eastern, perhaps Turkish, and in his mid-twenties. He clutched a small travel bag under his right arm as he waved with his left.

"Here's number four, coming our way." J.D. jerked his thumb out the door and checked with the pilot. "I'll get the door."

The pilot must have been in a hurry, too; he revved his twin engines to a throaty roar as soon as the latecomer tumbled in and J.D. pulled the outer door shut.

"Just move that lever down, sir, if you would, please," the pilot called over his shoulder without taking his eyes off the airplane's controls. J.D. was happy to comply.

"Hey, I've never been a stewardess before. Coffee? Tea?" The American grinned at the fourth passenger. But the handsome newcomer either didn't get the joke, or maybe he couldn't quite hear over the roar of the engines. He just nodded politely and settled into the other single seat, on the left and just behind the pilot.

"J.D. Roper, *PM Magazine,* New York. And you are. . . ?" J.D. held out his hand before taking his place in the backseat.

The other man seemed to consider the question for a moment, as if thinking of what to name himself.

"Tired. I am tired." With that the stranger closed his eyes, set his lips tightly, and settled back in his seat. He held tightly to his brown canvas bag, as if something alive might escape if he didn't.

"Do not disturb, huh?" J.D. chuckled and shrugged his shoulders. "Hey, no problem. I have plenty of sources who'd rather not see their names in the New York City phone book, if you know what I mean. Reminds me of an assignment I had in D.C. a couple years back, during the war, when I met this FBI agent. . . ."

J.D. went on with his story while the man next to him continued his work. Who was listening? Emily held on tightly as they took off with a chest-rattling roar, her head pressing back into the lumpy seat. She couldn't help staring as the island fell away below them, growing smaller and smaller as they banked left over the broad central plateau of Cyprus, then west toward the sparkling Mediterranean.

"And this guy, turns out he was working for the other side. . . ."

Only minutes later they were speeding over the ocean. Light powder blue deepened to sky blue, azure to indigo, royal to navy blue and every shade in between as the Mediterranean stretched out before and below them. The only sign of life Emily could make out was a fishing boat spreading lazy white wings among diamond whitecaps.

"Settle back and relax, gentlemen—er, *lady* and gentlemen," the pilot called back to them. "We'll be cruising at one hundred sixty-eight miles per hour with a tail wind, so we should be in Athens in four hours. We'll top off the tanks there and then continue on to Rome. I'll have you there by midafternoon, no problem. This old bird has a lot of miles left in her."

Emily hoped so. As fast as they were traveling, she decided that since she was stuck in a small plane without a washroom, it was probably a good thing she hadn't enjoyed an extra cup of tea that morning.

"Hmm. That's stange," the pilot mumbled to no one in particular and tapped a gauge on his control panel. He glanced quickly over his shoulder. Then he switched a couple of small levers back and forth several times.

What's he doing? Emily kept her eyes on the pilot, only a few feet in front of her. And she was still watching a few minutes later when a tiny movement caught her eye—the mystery man reaching into his bag, perhaps for a snack. Her stomach began to rumble at the thought. A sandwich sounded good just then.

But the dull silver glint of metal in the man's hand was no fig or orange. And the sleepy man's eyes had snapped open, instantly awake.

J.D. hadn't noticed. "And when I wrote this story, my editor, he just couldn't believe . . ."

Emily managed to catch his eye. His face turned pale and his words trailed off at the sight of the small, wicked-looking revolver. He slowly raised his hands and might have backed out the window if it had been open.

"Easy, pardner," he croaked. "Let's not get excited."

"Quiet, and don't move."

J.D. did as he was told, while the gray-haired man looked as if he would have a heart attack.

"Now, see here!" croaked the older man. But his eyes were as large as J.D.'s, and he made no move to stop what was going on.

Emily felt her heart in her throat as she looked down the stubby barrel of the weapon. Their pilot would be the last to know, with his back to them and the noise of the engines drowning out this gunman's threats.

"You can't quite see it right now," the pilot told them in a loud voice, "but way off to your right is the Turkish coast. And in less than a couple of hours, we'll be flying right over the island of Rhodes. At least . . ."

The pilot kept tapping on his instrument panel. At least what?

"What do you want?" asked J.D. "Money? We can talk. Just don't do anything stup—"

"I SAID, BE QUIET!" yelled the man. The veins in his neck stood out, and a bead of sweat rolled down his forehead.

Emily shivered in a nauseous wave of cold fear.

"Eh?" Their pilot glanced over his shoulder, but Emily almost wished he hadn't. At the sight of the hijacker, the pilot's face went almost as pale as J.D.'s. Even worse, their plane fell into a wobbly dive as the pilot's hands jerked and then froze on his butterfly-shaped steering wheel.

"Pull it back up!" demanded the hijacker. Like a cat, he somehow slipped into the empty copilot's seat and leveled his gun at the pilot. "Now!"

DANGER AT FIVE THOUSAND FEET

16

Emily tried not to scream as their plane tumbled. J.D. Roper looked as if he was going to be ill, and Emily would not have blamed him. The other passenger held on to his seat in wide-eyed surprise, until at last their plane leveled out once again.

"No more funny moves." The hijacker looked ready to use his gun, the way his finger quivered on the trigger. "Now, I want you to turn around and head for Lod airport, near Tel Aviv, heading one hundred thirty-four degrees. Increase speed to one hundred eighty-eight miles per hour, please."

Please? The word seemed to crash out of the sky without a parachute.

"This plane doesn't go that fast, and we're having a fuel problem." The pilot spoke through his teeth and gripped his steering wheel with white knuckles. "A bad gauge, I hope."

"Don't lie to me. I know all about this plane and your passengers: Mr. Roper. Miss Parkinson. Mr. Georgeopolis . . ."

Mr. Georgeopolis opened his mouth at the mention of his name but said nothing.

The hijacker went on. "And I know your top speed. Now, turn

us around, or I'll be glad to fly this plane myself."

Now that the hijacker had said more than two or three words, Emily could clearly make out the accent. He was Jewish!

The pilot made a long, slow loop to reverse course.

"Who are you, anyway?" J.D. broke the silence a few minutes later, once the color had started returning to his face. "And what do you want?"

"My name is none of your concern." Their hijacker's shark eyes never seemed to blink as he kept a close eye on his hostages—glancing from the pilot to the passengers and back again.

"But you obviously want something. How much do you want?"

"Fool!" The hijacker exploded. "If I had wanted money, I would have robbed a bank back in Tel Aviv."

"So you're from Tel Aviv?" J.D. pressed far past what Emily could have dared. "You owe us that much of an explanation."

"I owe you nothing, Mr. Roper! No explanations. You keep your mouth shut, and you'll live to tell your grandchildren about this adventure."

"All right then, mystery man. I'll tell you." J.D. jabbed at his palm, as if writing on an imaginary notebook. "You're with the Jewish Haganah—no, more radical than that. The Irgun, is that it? The Irgun stops at nothing. You've escaped from the camp, and you're in a big hurry to get back to Palestine, so much so you can't wait for your buddies to pick you up in a boat. How am I doing so far?"

The hijacker pulled his gun around to aim it at J.D.'s chest. Emily tried to keep her teeth from chattering, but it was no use. She could hardly watch.

"I'll bet you even knocked off somebody in the process, am I right?" J.D. must have been crazy to keep asking questions. Didn't the man have any sense?

The man's eyes narrowed. "If I hadn't already, you would be the first."

Amazingly, J.D. kept badgering the man over the next half hour. "Man, oh man. Keep talking. If the camp piece doesn't get me a Pulitzer, this one sure will. Let's see, 'Wild-eyed Jewish Terrorist Takes *PM* Reporter Hostage Over the Mediterranean.' This is great, absolutely great."

Great for you. Emily bit her lip. *The rest of us would like to survive, thank you very much.*

The hijacker ran his hand like a comb through his dark head of hair, obviously trying to decide what to do with the unstoppable American. Their pilot must have seen this as his chance; Emily looked away as he reached for his microphone. What could she do to help, without getting killed in the process?

"I think I'm going to be sick," she moaned, grabbing for the brown paper sack tucked under her seat. Perhaps it would be enough to pull the hijacker's attention away for just a moment while the pilot radioed for help. She leaned over and made a horrible, gut-wrenching sound.

"Mayday, mayday," she heard the pilot's voice. "This is Avro one-niner—"

"Give me that!" demanded the hijacker. He ripped the microphone out of the pilot's hand and yanked the end of the cord out of the radio before he tossed it to the floor. "There will be no communication from this airplane! No radio, and"—he leveled his glare at J.D.—"no magazine articles."

Roper stared right back at the hijacker, trading steel for steel. "You can break the radio, friend. But writing is what I do. So pry my cold fingers off my pencil if you want to."

The hijacker glared at them for a moment, then left the pilot's side and quickly slid back to face them. He grabbed the empty airsick bag from Emily's hands and threw it at her face.

She didn't flinch. But something inside her clicked just then. Maybe it was the example of the cheeky American.

"Is this how a Jew returns to the Promised Land?" she blurted out in Hebrew. "Hiding behind a hostage? Behind a gun?"

Emily gasped at what had just tumbled past her lips, and for the first time since they'd left Cyprus, the hijacker seemed almost startled. But only for a moment.

"Ah," he answered back. "Your Hebrew is quite good."

"I . . ." Emily's face flushed, and she shrank back from his glare. "I didn't mean . . ."

"What's this? What are you two saying?" J.D. paused and looked at them with a puzzled expression. "In English, if you don't mind."

"Forget it." The hijacker kept his gun raised as he switched back to English. "You listen, and I'll tell you something. In fact, I'll tell you exactly why our people are sitting behind barbed wire in that camp back there on Cyprus. Does your magazine want to know *that*?"

But the hijacker's speech was interrupted by a sharp buzz and the flash of a red warning light.

"What's that?" he shouted, turning quickly to the pilot. "No tricks!"

"I tried to tell you," the pilot repeated as he shook his head and pointed to a gauge. "We must have developed a fuel leak somehow right after takeoff. It looks like we're almost out of gas. We're going to need to land in a hurry.

"There's the coast," he said, pointing to a low smudge on the horizon. "Where do you want me to put down?"

Emily closed her eyes and sighed at the sight of the land she'd almost never expected to see again. She didn't need to see the pilot's strained face to know they were almost out of fuel.

The hijacker managed a tight-lipped smile. "Our destination

hasn't changed. Land at Lod airport, outside Tel Aviv."

"What?" Their pilot managed a questioning look. A deserted road, perhaps, or a stretch of desert flatland. But the airport?

"You heard me."

"Yes, but when I land, they're going to be all over us. Control doesn't appreciate it when a plane drops in without clearance."

A man's voice over the radio two minutes later proved the pilot's point.

"I repeat," crackled the radio. "Identify yourself. Incoming aircraft, you are not, I say, *not* cleared for landing!"

Emily glanced at the microphone and wire, still on the floor where the hijacker had thrown them after he had ripped them out of the radio. They could hear the control tower but couldn't talk back if they'd wanted to.

"It doesn't matter," said the hijacker. "This is the place. I have friends waiting for me."

Emily wondered what kind of "friends" this man might have and hoped she wouldn't have to meet them.

"Heading down, then," reported their pilot. Everyone buckled their lap belts, even the hijacker in the copilot's seat.

The rest of the flight was a white-knuckled blur to Emily as they practically fell out of the sky, coming in low over some gray metal hangars, and bumping down twice before the tail finally settled to the ground with a rude thump.

"Sorry," mumbled the pilot. Emily didn't blame him.

"Over there." The hijacker pointed toward a crowd of men and a couple of airport trucks, and they taxied closer. "Everyone will stay in the plane until I am gone, or—"

Or what? He still had his gun.

Red lights flashing, one of the trucks approached, and the plane's engines shut down with a sputter. Perhaps they had run out of gas on the spot.

"How's that?" asked the pilot, but their hijacker ignored the question. Instead he shoved open the door and vaulted out to the pavement.

"*Shalom,* Emily Parkinson."

Peace? An odd word coming from the mouth of a man with a gun. But by this time his weapon was again tucked into his bag. Emily watched as he met the first men coming toward them and pointed back at their plane. From there he hurried on and climbed into the cab of a waiting truck, idling just around the corner of the nearby hangar.

"Where's the emergency?" shouted the first airport worker to reach them. "Who's hurt?"

"No!" J.D. was the first one down the steps.

"But your friend there said—"

"No, you don't understand. He's no friend. That guy's a hijacker!"

He pointed to where the truck had been, but it was already too late. The hijacker and his partners had disappeared with a squealing of tires in a cloud of smoke. They must have been waiting for him.

In the confusion that followed, a team of military police surrounded the plane, though of course they weren't going to find the hijacker now. But never mind him. Emily had a new plan.

If I can just get back to Jerusalem . . . She backed quietly away from the gathering crowd, valise in hand. *Daddy and Mum are sure to be there.*

"Pardon me." She stopped a young soldier who had just pulled up in a jeep. "But I must get to Jerusalem right away. My father is—"

The soldier listened carefully to her story before he got on his radio. He knew of a convoy leaving that afternoon, he said, and circumstances being as they were, he thought he could find her a seat.

And J.D. Roper? Emily had no doubt he would probably win the prize he'd talked so constantly about. As she left the runway with the young soldier, she looked back to see the American had found a new audience for his latest tale.

HOME NO MORE
17

"You say you've been out of the country?" The square-jawed young corporal beside her was apparently a friend of the soldier she'd first asked for help back at the airport. He drove his truck with one hand, leaned the other elbow out the open window, and chewed gum nonstop.

"Only for a few days." But it might as well have been a life-time; so much had changed in that short time.

Emily's driver nodded knowingly. "So why in . . . pardon me, why would you want to come back 'ere, I'd like to ask? And wot 'appened to yer parents?"

"They're in Jerusalem." Emily tried to explain as much as she could one more time. "I tried to telephone, but the lines weren't working."

"Ah, mostly they're down. We have to use the radio."

"I see."

As long as she found her parents, how she reached them didn't matter much to Emily. And it certainly didn't matter that the usu-ally forty-five-minute drive from the airstrip to Jerusalem would eventually take over three hours. Security delays, the soldiers called it. In the end they would make it to Jerusalem, unlike the Jews who had tried so many times in past days—and failed. Emily tried her best not to stare at the burned-out hulks of dozens of transport and supply trucks lining the highway on both sides.

"So many," she whispered. The wind ruffled her hair as they rumbled up the hill. A well-armed jeep and two army personnel carriers led the way, then their truck, then three more trucks behind. Each was decked out with a bright blue, red, and white Union Jack flag. There was no chance anyone would mistake the drivers for Jews.

"Eh, what?"

"I said, there are so many more wrecks than I remember. Where did they all come from?"

The corporal steered around a pothole as if the wreckage was just part of the landscape. "I s'pose it's been getting a bit intense these past few days. The Jews rounded up a few trucks, tried to bring in supplies from the coast. And the Arabs up there"—he jerked a thumb at the hilltops—"hide in those villages and just rained down a few shots."

He showed her with his hand how he thought the attacks had come. Emily looked away as they passed another skeleton of a truck, charred completely black. Its windshield had been entirely shattered.

"Looks a bit more than a few shots, as you say. Can't you protect them?"

The corporal chewed his gum and shrugged. "Only so much we can do for people bound and determined to get themselves into a donnybrook, if you know my meaning."

Emily frowned. She was afraid she did know. She gazed up at the gathering purple shadows on the surrounding hills up to Jerusalem. She had taken this way dozens of times, but it always took her breath away. Even more now, with the wrecks and the faintly charred smell of burning rubber. She squirmed on the cracked vinyl seat under the feeling of having so many eyes watching their military convoy.

"They're watching?"

"Don't worry, miss. Those blighters won't bother us none. It's just Jewish traffic they're after. We're bulletproof."

Bulletproof? Hardly. But in a way she supposed he was right. The Arabs surely wouldn't attack the British. Still, it didn't make her feel any better to see robed men in the distance with long machine guns and rifles slung over their shoulders, standing in profile on the hilltops. A couple of them even waved down at them.

Worse yet, the driver waved back.

"Jerusalem up ahead." He pointed with his chin as they continued on their way. Emily sat on the edge of her seat until they finally pulled up to Ben Yehuda Street, near her home.

"That's close enough, thank you." Emily held on as the truck screeched to a halt.

"You're sure?"

"Of course." She gave the soldier a smile. "I can walk the last few blocks. I want to surprise Daddy."

"Well . . ." He glanced around the empty neighborhood and rubbed his chin. "I suppose it looks safe enough right now. You'll go straight home, then?"

"My house is just over there, Corporal. Just around the corner. I promise I'll go straight there."

"Corporal *Jennings*." He tossed back a friendly salute. "And it's the least I could do for the major's daughter. You'll mention it to him, eh?"

"Of course. Thank you again, Corporal Jennings." Emily did her best to sound sure of herself. As soon as her feet hit the street, the truck rumbled back in the direction they had come from. It disappeared through a cloud of choking black smoke.

Why didn't I tell him to wait? What if Daddy has already moved out, and . . . no. He said he was going to be here right until the end.

Yes, he would be there to the end. It was his duty, after all. Only a few weeks remained in the British Mandate until the British were scheduled to leave Palestine. And if there was one thing the British were good at, it was schedules. Her father would be home by precisely six-ten, and it was at least that. If Mother had been able to catch a flight out of the country, he would be sitting in the house all alone. Emily quickened her pace, past the flowering tangerine tree with the heavenly scent, past the corner. . . .

Emily's feet betrayed her; they would not move another step, and she stood glued to the sidewalk. If she had not grown up in this house, if she had not slept every night for the past eight years in the bedroom over the welcoming entryway, she would not have believed it was the same building. Even so, something told her she'd made a horrible mistake—walked down the wrong street, turned the wrong corner.

"No!" she gasped. Emily would have stepped up through the massive oak door that once opened into their front den—if it had still hung in its place. She would have pounded on the windows and wakened her father—if any windows had remained. She would have run back into the home that had once held so many good memories for her—if only there were more to it than a charred shell.

"It can't be!"

But it was. A red ribbon fluttered across the gaping hole where the front door had once been—the only barrier between the street and an ashen black cave. She could not look. Instead, she turned and ran, fleeing the ghost of her old home, trying to shake the cruel picture that now snagged her memory like a burr on a sock.

But where's Daddy? Surely he would have survived the disaster.

But she didn't want to think about that, either.

So she ran toward the only other place where she might find shelter: Anthony and Rachel's house.

Emily halfway expected her aunt and uncle's comfortable white stucco home to look the same as hers. So she held her breath before creeping up through the Yemin Moshe neighborhood.

Finally she allowed herself to relax. Yes, the neighborhood had seen happier days. Here and there windows were boarded over, and some doorways even had sandbags piled around them for protection. But a few brave yellow flowers still bloomed from cheerful window boxes at Number 3 Malki Street.

"Thank you, Lord," Emily whispered. She could only take so much. She stood just outside the Mediterranean-style entry, finishing her quiet prayer, when she heard a snuffling sound from under the door.

Mfff, mffff.

The snuffling grew louder, followed by a yip and a wild scratching. For the first time in this long, horrible day, Emily could laugh at something—the welcoming sniff of her Great Dane, Julian.

"Julian, is it really you?" Emily fell to her knees and poked her fingers under the door. The snuffling turned to a full-powered howl, enough to catch the attention of the entire Yemin Moshe neighborhood, not to mention anyone inside the home.

"What on earth?" A woman's voice came closer from behind the door. "Julian, you were just outside. Is there a cat out there?"

When the door flew open, for once Emily didn't mind being bowled over by a very large dog. Julian may have been too old to travel back to England and to see much through his clouded eyes, but his sense of smell was as keen as ever. And he seemed instantly ready to forgive Emily for abandoning him eleven days ago.

"Anthony, come here!" cried Emily's aunt Rachel. "It's . . . it's . . ."

"It's me." Emily looked up from under the dog with a hopeful grin.

"Well, look what the dog dragged in!" Uncle Anthony seemed almost as happy as Julian to see her. He dropped the coil of rope he was carrying and stared. But then reality set in. "Wait a moment. What are you doing here? You're supposed to be on your way to London! Your father said he'd arranged for everything!"

Emily nodded. No matter how hard she tried, she couldn't keep the tears from her eyes.

"It's a long story. But—Father and Mum, what happened to *them*? And what happened to our house?"

"Oh dear." Aunt Rachel pulled Emily to her feet and helped dust her off. "So you've seen the place, have you? I can tell we have a lot of catching up to do. So much has happened in the short time since you left."

Uncle Anthony must have understood the horrible question in Emily's eyes, since he rested his hand on her shoulder as they stepped inside.

"They're fine, Emily. Your mother and father are fine. They're just not here in Jerusalem."

Emily looked back at him in surprise.

"Your mother was supposed to fly to England shortly after you left, but—"

"She got a flight?"

"It was delayed several times until yesterday morning." Aunt Rachel cleared another coil of rope and a four-foot pile of blankets off the couch so they could sit down. "I think she's on her way now. And then the fire bomb . . . that was the day before yesterday.

Your father was reassigned to Haifa, I think. I don't quite know the details. It's all happened so fast."

"But why didn't they tell me?"

"Oh, I'm sure they would have. But they thought you were on your way home to England. I'm sure your mother wanted to tell you in person. There was no need to worry you."

"Worry *me*?" Emily's voice trailed off. If her parents only knew what she had just been through!

"Yes, well, things will turn out all right. I'm sorry about the mess."

Emily looked around at the living room for the first time. Normally straight and tidy, the room looked like an emergency shelter after an earthquake, with cots and blankets set up wall to wall. Aunt Rachel waved her hand at the mess.

"But as you can see, at the moment we're preparing for a few guests."

"A few guests!" When Uncle Anthony laughed, he sounded exactly like his older brother, Emily's father. "That's her American humor."

"I wish it were a joke. Would you look at this mess? Everything always seems to happen at the same time."

"Thanks to your friend Dov." Uncle Anthony smiled slightly.

"Dov?" Emily's mind raced to catch up. Seeing her former home now destroyed, discovering her parents were gone, and now . . . What had she returned to?

MISSION TO THE WALL

18

"Absolutely not." Uncle Anthony put his fork down after dinner the next day. "You've already been through so much."

"But you need help." Emily wasn't giving up so easily. "You can't carry a dozen little girls across the valley by yourself. Especially not with all those Arab guards down there."

"I won't be alone. And as I said, we don't know precisely how many orphans we're talking about."

"Then what *do* we know?"

"I'm afraid the details were fairly vague. Dov did his best, but his broadcast was short."

"Broadcast?"

"Mm-hmm, and that's just it: We have to assume that anyone in Jerusalem with a radio receiver could have overheard our conversations."

"Oh dear."

"Now you're sounding just like your aunt." Uncle Anthony shook his head but offered a small grin. "But listen, we do know that Dov needs our help and that he's going to try to escape the Jewish Quarter with the orphans."

Emily studied her uncle to make sure he wasn't kidding, and he turned the questioning look back at her.

"What?" he asked.

"It's just all so surprising." She scratched her head. "Dov helping orphans?"

"You have to remember he's one, too." Aunt Rachel caught herself too late. Emily had told them about Cyprus. "Or rather, he *thinks* he is."

"Still." Emily wrinkled her nose. "It just doesn't seem quite like something Dov would help with, let alone plan."

"Emily!" Her aunt scolded her. "That's no way to talk about your friend. People do change, you know."

Even so, Emily wondered as her uncle went on. *Has Dov changed that much? He didn't used to care about anyone.*

"The rescue's to be tonight, as far as I can tell. Over the wall, near the Church of the Dormition."

"Won't that be terribly dangerous?" Emily tried not to gasp.

"Exactly why I don't want you involved," Uncle Anthony said. "And dangerous or not, we must get those children to safety." He crossed his arms. "You've probably heard that attacks on the Old City are getting worse every night. It's deplorable."

"But where are the attacks coming from?"

Uncle Anthony shrugged. "It changes daily, but mostly from the south. Look down in the Hinnom Valley; you'll always see Arab patrols. And what are the British authorities doing about it? I'll tell you: Nothing. Absolutely nothing."

He paced like a caged lion. "They've already got their tickets home to London. What do they care that people are being killed?"

"Anthony." Aunt Rachel tried to calm her husband. "Your brother."

"My brother is . . ." He bit his lip. "He's probably concerned about his daughter. I'd feel much better if we could get word to him. We'll just have to keep trying."

"I'll be all right, Uncle Anthony." Emily tried her best to keep her voice from cracking with worry.

"Oh, I know you will. Especially if you stay here tonight, with all the doors locked, while—"

"Alone? Please, I can't do that. You simply *must* take me along."

"No, Emily."

"Oh, but I shan't be in the way. And I could help with the little ones."

The least of these my brethren. Emily couldn't forget the words: *"Inasmuch as ye have done it unto one of the least of these my brethren, ye have done it unto me."*

But her uncle wouldn't budge.

"I don't think so."

"Wouldn't it help to have someone along who could speak a little Arabic, just in case?"

Uncle Anthony still shook his head, but Emily could tell he was thinking about it. She didn't tell him her Arabic wasn't good at all, but she usually did know enough to get by.

"Tell me one thing again, though, Uncle Anthony."

He raised his eyebrows.

"Are you *sure* we're talking about the same Dov?"

Four hours later Emily looked up at the star-filled Jerusalem sky over her aunt and uncle's home, searching for any moonlight that would betray them.

"All right." Uncle Anthony looked around at their little group of radio technicians and broadcasters, people who had helped them with the Jewish Haganah radio station in their home. "I know this isn't quite what you signed up for. But sometimes you do what you have to do."

"Hey, you want muscles?" A man named Avi flexed his biceps and smiled a crooked, toothy grin. "I've got muscles."

Everyone laughed, and Anthony rested his hand on Emily's shoulder.

"You all know our niece, Emily. She's going to be with me and Rachel at the wall, helping with the kids. Eliahu, you're the lookout. Any sign of an Arab with a weapon, you know what to do. And you fellows"—he pointed to Avi and another college student—"you're going to be cranking us over the valley. Avi from Mount Zion, and Tristan from the other end of the cable in the hospital. Don't leave us hanging."

Tristan gave them a grin and a smart salute. "You can count on us, Anthony—I mean, sir. Pulling secret cable cars across the Hinnom Valley in the middle of the night is our specialty."

Emily liked the way this Tristan fellow helped ease some of the night's tension. But she still couldn't keep her knees from knocking. Uncle Anthony, on the other hand, didn't help matters much.

"My brother's never going to speak to me again if he finds out what you're doing tonight," he told Emily a minute later. "Of course, perhaps that's not such a bad thing."

"Uncle Anthony!"

"Just teasing. I must admit it's good to have you back. But you must promise me you will be careful. Otherwise, he'll have an even *better* reason not to speak to me."

With that they collected their ropes and headed out the door.

"Father, bring them over the wall safely," Emily heard Anthony whispering, "just as you did Joshua and his men."

Dov looked right, then left, then right again. Finally he signaled for the others to follow.

One by one the orphan girls came scurrying his way: Kiva, Frieda, Chava. He counted eleven. Where was the last one?

He was about to run back to the ruined building near the wall when he saw his brother coming toward him—the missing girl under his right arm.

Natan!

Dov almost grinned, but it was too early for celebration. He adjusted the ragged coil of rope that dug into his neck and shoulder. Soon they'd see if his plan would work.

"Couldn't get this one to move her legs," Natan whispered as he set down little Batya with the others. He squatted and looked his brother in the eye.

"What are you doing here, Natan? I thought—"

"Yeah, well. When I came looking for you, the Liebermans told me what you were doing. You're crazy."

"Is that what you came here to tell me?"

"Not exactly."

"Then what?"

"Well, you once risked your neck to get me into the Old City." Natan studied his shoes. "I suppose the least I can do is help get you out of here."

He didn't wait for Dov to respond, but turned to growl at the knot of young orphans.

"Hey, unless you want to stay here with me the rest of your lives, you're going to do what this guy tells you. Understand?"

They nodded seriously; they had already promised Dov to be good. Batya started to cry.

Dov sighed. *This isn't going to be as easy as I'd thought.*

Getting up on the top of the wall wasn't the hard part. Dov helped Frieda step up behind the crumbled home and onto the roof. He had rehearsed it in his head dozens of times, ever since he first found the spot.

"I'm scared." Frieda had frozen to a spot on the roof and would not budge.

"Sure you are. We all are." Dov tried to drag her.

But she would not be comforted and dug in her heels as she set up a sobbing that threatened to turn worse.

What would Joshua have done in this situation?

"Frieda, please," Dov pleaded. "We have to be quiet or they'll hear us. You don't want that, do you?"

Frieda stuck out her lip and shook her head no, but she would not let Dov take her hand.

"Here you go." Natan swept in behind her and lifted the girl off her feet. She didn't seem to mind as he passed her up to the top of the wall.

"Now comes the fun part," he whispered.

Dov nodded and tied a quick double loop at the end of his rope. There would be no basket.

Like climbing a tall tree, getting down was the hard part. It would be hard enough to get a dozen petrified orphans safely down to the other side. But getting them down without anyone seeing them would be next to impossible—or so it seemed to Dov. Of course, he wasn't about to tell that to anyone else at this point. Not now.

"All right, now, listen to me. Quit your whimpering." Dov tried to gather them around in a huddle and keep them low and away from the edge of the wall so no one would see them. He took a deep breath.

"So here's what we're going to do. Each one of you is going to take a turn on the swing. We're going to lower you down, you're going to take the loops off, and then you're going to run for that doorway over there. Someone will be waiting for you. Do you understand me?"

Most of the girls nodded.

"But that sounds scary." Frieda looked as if she might melt down in panic.

"It's not scary," Natan assured them.

But first they had to wait as a pair of men below them strolled past in no particular hurry. The question was, how soon would they be coming back? One of the girls whimpered, almost like a puppy locked in a shed.

"What will those men do to us if they find us?" asked Frieda.

"I don't know." Dov readied his rope. "But believe me, you don't want to find out."

As soon as the men were out of range, it was time for the first drop: Frieda. Dov tightened the twin loops around her waist and legs and took her to the edge.

"Close your eyes if you have to," he told her, and then with barely a sound they lowered girl number one over the edge.

She tumbled only a little when they got her all the way to the ground. The moment she touched down, two figures immediately emerged from the shadows of the tall Dormition gateway. One Dov recognized as Anthony Parkinson. And the other . . .

Could it be?

A DOZEN DOWN

19

"Emily?" When Dov whispered, it was hardly loud enough to hear down on the ground. Despite the waning moon, it wasn't light enough to see anyone clearly. No, she was safely home in England by now. It had to be someone else.

"Come on." Natan shook his brother's shoulder. "We still have eleven more to go."

They did, and the process of lowering a dozen girls forty feet down the side of an ancient city wall was painfully slow—slower still when Arab guards strolled by every few minutes. At least for tonight, the British were nowhere in sight.

"Why aren't they home in bed?" whispered Natan. He hefted an orange-sized rock in the palm of his hand and peeked over the edge.

Dov grabbed his collar. "Don't get any ideas." Dov had caught a glimpse of the rifles the men carried under their flowing robes. Surely Natan had, too, despite the darkness. "It would be the last rock you'd ever drop."

"Yeah, yeah." Natan frowned and set down the stone. He had

to know his brother was right. "Remind me again why I'm doing this?"

"Because it's the right thing to do."

"And since when did you know about doing the right thing?"

"Since . . ." Dov shrugged. "I don't know. I'm learning."

His brother was probably right to wonder. This plan was dangerous, but Dov also knew this *was* the right thing. It had to be. Because for once, he was totally focused on what somebody *else* needed. Not just himself.

Besides, he was sure it was what Mr. Bin-Jazzi would have done. And if anybody knew the right thing to do, it was Bible-quoting Farouk Bin-Jazzi.

"Watch it." Natan gave the rope a turn around his fist, but still it slipped. It had already frayed a bit where it ran over the wall's edge. "This rope isn't going to hold too many more people."

"Doesn't need to." Dov checked to see if the twelfth girl had made it to safety. "Stop the bus. Here's where I get off."

"You're sure you want to do this?"

Dov's stomach tightened. After all this time searching for his brother, now he was going to just leave him here? But there was no time for thinking, only time enough to pull the rope up, secure the end around himself, and get ready for the last drop.

"Here, don't forget this." Natan handed across the radio transmitter in its small suitcase. "Wouldn't want your Haganah friends to get mad at you for losing their radio, eh?"

Dov took a deep breath and took the suitcase handle.

"All right." Natan stuck out his hand. "I'm not good at good-byes."

"Me neither."

"If you ever want to see your long-lost brother again, just put out a call on your old radio, eh? It worked before."

Dov smiled. "Sure. I'll do that. Meet me at the windmill by Anthony and Rachel's."

"Maybe somewhere else. I have a feeling I may not be able to reach the windmill any time soon."

The thought didn't make Dov feel better.

Natan finally grabbed his brother in a brief, awkward bear hug. "Go on. You'd better get going, before—"

"I know, I know." Dov had already coaxed a dozen others over the edge to safety. He could certainly make the same drop himself.

"I've got you." The muscles on Natan's strong arms bulged as he paid out rope one more time. Dov crawled over the top of the wall backward and tried not to crush his suitcase in the process.

"You weigh a ton!" grunted Natan. "Not like those girls."

But despite his weight, Dov didn't drop as easily. In the process of clinging to the rope and hanging on to his radio, the rope started twisting around his ankle.

"Hold it!" he hissed as he worked to free himself. That took only a moment, but Natan had troubles of his own. Dov fell a couple of feet, then jerked and hung.

I'm going to fall!

Not quite. He bobbed on the rope like a marionette, and there was nothing he could do to come down faster or more slowly.

"The rope's breaking!" Natan whispered.

Dov would rather have heard just about anything else. He heard a scramble from behind and below. And when he glanced down, he guessed he was only a meter or so from the stone pavement.

It was far enough. When the rope finally parted, he tumbled down and backward. He hit first the flat of his heels, then rolled back on his tailbone before bumping into something soft.

"Oh!" cried a girl, and it echoed against the walls. They both fell in a heap—Dov, the girl, and his radio. He held it up as best he could, trying not to fall on it.

"Are you all right?" asked the girl. By that time Dov was sure who it was. Even in the darkness he knew he had just fallen on Emily Parkinson.

How she came to be standing under the Old City wall this midnight had to be a long story, best told another time. At least he was pretty sure he hadn't broken any bones; everything worked.

Emily pulled him up by his shoulders just in time to face a pair of angry-looking men.

Emily could barely see their faces behind the traditional white Arab *kaffiyeh* headgear. But she was certain of one thing.

They were not smiling.

"Matha tafal al-an?" shouted one. "What are you doing?"

Emily tried to back away, inch by inch. And she squinted when one of the men snapped on a flashlight and beamed the bright light on her face. The other man kept an ancient rifle pointed at her and Dov, and she had no desire to see if the blunderbuss actually worked.

"We were just, eh, we were just leaving." Emily thought she used the right Arabic words.

"Emily," hissed Dov. "We need to—"

"Keep quiet, Dov," she whispered out of the side of her mouth. "I think I can talk us out of this."

"No, you can't."

"Shh."

"You don't understand, Emily."

"Quiet!" ordered the taller of the two men. "The bag. Let's see it."

He pointed to the battered suitcase Dov had lugged along with him. She wondered what could be so important that it would be worth smuggling over the wall.

"Just show them your suitcase, Dov. They want to see it."

"No, that's the problem," he murmered back. "I can't. We're in big trouble if I do."

"We're in big trouble if you *don't*."

She hoped the men didn't understand their exchange. So far, they didn't appear to. She tried not to jump as the gate latch clicked behind them. But it was too loud not to hear.

"Eh?" The man with the gun began to turn, just as the pavement exploded and rock shards splattered in all directions. A war cry sounded from the top of the wall.

Had a bomb landed at their feet? Strong hands grabbed Emily from behind.

"Emily!" Uncle Anthony shouted. "This way!"

The man with the rifle looked both ways—up and behind. In that split instant of chaos he must have decided the attack from above was the more serious. And in that split second of chaos, Emily could see a man standing on top of the wall, outlined clearly against the night sky.

"Natan!" Dov shouted up at a dark figure. "Look out!"

Too late. The rifleman had already taken aim. Emily screamed at the flash of light and deadly thunder. Almost in slow motion, she saw the man spin around and jerk like a rag doll before he tumbled off the far side.

"No!" Dov began to lunge for the shooter, but Anthony already had a hand on his collar. Before Emily could be sure of what had really happened, he dragged them back into the church courtyard, slammed the door, and drove home the bolt.

"Come! There's no time." Anthony herded them through a

narrow maze of passageways, past dark, looming church buildings and courtyards.

But Dov kept looking back. "My brother. Didn't you see he was shot? I have to help him."

But Emily knew there was nothing to do, no way to help. They heard an explosion of gunfire, followed by the groan of a splintering wood door. What else could it be but the door coming down behind them?

"I'm very sorry, Dov." Anthony wouldn't let them slow down for a moment. "There's nothing we can do for Natan now. Not from this side of the wall."

As if to prove the point, a chorus of angry shouts now followed them through the maze.

"You kids go on ahead." He stopped in his tracks. "You know where the tramway is, Emily. Avi is waiting for us there."

But Emily wouldn't let go of her uncle. It would not be that easy.

"No!" She held to his shirt. "We have to stick together. You said so yourself!"

"Emily, please!"

But she didn't let go. Her uncle turned his head as if to test the wind, then paused a moment before changing his mind.

"All right. But we must hurry!"

That might have been easier if they hadn't turned down a dead-end alley next to the church's graveyard. A locked iron gate barred the way between them and a dark forest of stone crosses.

"Back!" cried Uncle Anthony.

Emily almost couldn't. The shouts and footsteps of their pursuers grew louder every moment.

THE LEAST OF
THESE

20

Emily's lungs burned for air, her side ached, and they still hadn't found their way out of the maze of pathways surrounding the old Dormition Church. They turned left around a wall, hurrying to stay ahead of the shouts behind them.

This way? she wondered, pausing at the end of a lane. Dov nearly bowled her over as they stumbled out into a hard-dirt playing field where students probably played soccer during the day. It seemed so odd right then running across a goal line.

But they were running for their lives, not for a ball.

Emily retraced the steps they had taken earlier that evening, across the playing field and down the olive-studded hillside. Was it her imagination, or were the shouts growing fainter? She couldn't be sure, and she surely didn't want to stop to find out.

They turned to follow the brow of the hill, and she knew they were almost directly across from her aunt and uncle's home in Yemin Moshe. Below them, in the Hinnom Valley, dozens of their pursuers' friends probably slept. Or waited.

"Here." Uncle Anthony finally turned aside behind a thicket of three trees.

"Are we going to hide in here?" Dov asked. "Are you sure that's a good—"

"Shh." Emily clapped a hand over Dov's mouth and pointed, hoping he would see. Avi had done a good job of hiding the tram in the bushes.

Dov did his best to make out what Emily was pointing at, but it was like looking at a strange puzzle for the first time. He could easily have walked right by without seeing a thing. In the dark, all he saw was a thicket of bushes. Just a thicket of bushes . . . maybe with a cable leading out the side, into the darkness, over the valley? He took another step as Anthony and his friend tore off a covering of olive branches and brambles.

"Step aboard," whispered Anthony, and Emily seemed to know where to go. "Hurry."

Step aboard what?

A moment later Dov was crouching in the front of a small metal hanging tram about the size of a rowboat and attached to a stout overhead cable by several well-greased wheels.

"What *is* this thing?" he wondered aloud.

"Shh." Emily didn't explain right away, only put a finger to her lips and pointed down at the darkness that was the Hinnom Valley. He couldn't see ten feet in any direction, only guessed what might lie below. She looked back at the load of quiet passengers, and when Anthony tapped lightly on the side of the tram, she picked up a flashlight and blinked twice into the darkness.

"Hold on," she whispered, and the tram rocked in the cool darkness as another cable on the valley side took up slack and began to pull them across.

"The girls?" Dov asked. After all, they were his responsibility, in a way.

"They're fine," answered Avi. "We brought them across in two quick loads, they were so light. They'll be waiting for us."

"That's enough." Anthony silenced them from where he crouched low in the back of the tram, out of sight. From then on all Dov could hear was the quiet whisper of the oiled wheels. At least they'd managed to lose the attackers back at the church.

Now his stomach told him they were hanging high above the Hinnom Valley—how high, he wasn't sure. He held on until they came closer to a tall building built into the hillside. He wasn't sure he had noticed it before.

"Almost there." Emily was the first to break the silence as they glided closer, then finally cleared the valley and were pulled into a small opening in the basement of the building.

"Welcome to the other side." A man Dov didn't recognize stepped away from a large crank and helped them out.

This is a dream, Dov decided as he stepped into a small basement room. A dream, like the nightmarish years of growing up in the camps of Nazi Germany. A dream, all of it: Dropping the orphans over the wall. The scuffle with the Arabs. His brother falling in the darkness. Emily and the chase through the grounds of the Church of the Dormition. This make-believe ride across the dark Valley of Hinnom.

All a dream, and now the girls crowding around him were part of the dream, too. Little Batya grabbed his hand as they followed Anthony out of the building. In the morning Dov would wake up and all this would be gone. Convinced of this, he shuffled behind Emily up the hill toward Number 3 Malki Street.

For a moment Emily wondered if she would have to carry Dov the rest of the way to her aunt and uncle's house. She looked back at him once more.

"Are you sure you're all right, Dov?"

He didn't answer, just walked. Two of the youngest orphan girls had latched on to his arms as if he were their big brother, but he didn't seem to mind.

Is that the Dov I knew? she wondered, and her mind wandered back to the island. There would be plenty of time later to tell him about his mother and to give him the letter Mrs. Zalinski had written. For now it was enough that Dov's orphans were safe.

The least of these.

And they could all use a good night's sleep.

"You did the right thing, Dov." Uncle Anthony rested his hand on Dov's shoulder. "There's not a doubt in my mind."

What was this? The sunlight had pried Dov's eyes open too early. And Julian hadn't helped with his wet kisses.

"Mmmfff." Dov turned his head away and wiped his cheek on the pillowcase. Was the familiar Parkinson sofa part of his dream, too?

But dreams couldn't hurt like this. The memory of Natan falling from the top of the wall had played itself over and over in Dov's half sleep, more times than he wanted to count. At least with a dream, he could have taken comfort in knowing it was not real.

Now he had grown tired of trying to fool himself. This was real—too real, right down to the last cruel memory. He forced open his eyes.

"I don't think he heard you." Emily sat in the living room, too, and everyone was dressed. What time was it?

"I heard you," he mumbled. "And yeah, I brought your transmitter back."

"That's not what I meant." Anthony settled on the sofa arm by Dov's feet. "Although I do appreciate what you did with the radio. You did some good work in there, Dov."

"Hmm."

"I meant that you did the right thing, bringing those girls out of the Old City."

"Oh that."

"Yes that. Even though . . ."

Even though what? Dov wanted to scream. *Go ahead, say it!*

"Dov, we're very sorry about your brother."

"I didn't ask him to do that." The tears began to soak Dov's pillow. "He didn't have to come along. He *shouldn't* have come along."

"But he did." Anthony's voice felt like a warm blanket over Dov's shoulders, though Dov would never have said so. "That was his decision. I'm just saying *you* did the right thing, getting those orphans out. The right thing."

"I don't know." Dov took a jagged breath. "Maybe it was my fault that Natan—"

"It was *not* your fault, Dov Zalinski," Emily interrupted. "Do you hear me? Everybody knows it wasn't your fault."

"Still . . ." Dov protested.

No one said anything else, as if daring him to continue. Fine. He would tell them. He propped himself up on one elbow.

"Listen, for the first time in my life, I thought I was doing something decent. Maybe even . . ." Dov sighed. "I don't know . . . for God. And then *this* had to happen to my brother."

"I wish that hadn't happened, too." Anthony ran a hand through his hair. "But just because everything didn't turn out exactly the way you planned, that doesn't mean God wasn't in it,

Dov. And it certainly doesn't mean what happened to Natan was your fault."

"I don't know." This was too confusing. Dov wanted to bury his face in the pillow once more to make it all go away.

"I'm sorry, too, Dov." It was Emily's turn. "But I think Uncle Anthony is right. Look at how you helped all those orphans. God used you, don't you think? In a good way, I mean."

"Wait a minute." Dov's eyes snapped open. "What *did* happen to the girls, anyway?"

"We took them to a couple of neighbors' houses for the night. They'll be fine, if we can find them something to eat."

Dov's stomach growled on cue.

"Did I hear someone mention food?" Aunt Rachel came out of the kitchen with a towel in her hands and a smile on her face.

"Breakfast?" Anthony looked hopeful.

"Well, there's not much food in this neighborhood, either. But I can offer you some gourmet sardines and some coffee."

The coffee would taste like Jerusalem mud and the bait fish swam in tin-flavored red sauce, but just about anything sounded good. And when Dov rolled over to think about it, Julian took his chance to pull away from Emily and plant another kiss on Dov's cheek.

"Ohh." Dov jerked his head back again. "That dog of yours!"

"Mine?" Emily dared to grin. "I thought he was *yours* now."

"I was only baby-sitting him until you got back. Now you're back. But . . . what *are* you doing here? I thought you were on your way back to England."

"I was."

"So how did you come back? I mean, why?"

Emily paused for a moment to pull a letter out of her small backpack.

"I suppose you could say I came back to deliver a letter. Only,

I wasn't expecting to do it this way at all. Maybe God had other plans."

"Sounds familiar." Dov nodded.

"Go on; take it. It's for you. From someone you know."

Finally Dov took the wrinkled blue envelope, and his fingers trembled as he turned it around between his fingers. A faint hand had written in precise, flowing letters across the front. *To my son Dov.*

Dov closed his eyes as the words hit him full force. It almost didn't matter what the note said, only whom it was from. *Imma!* Could it be? Was it really? By this time his hands trembled too much to open the flap.

"Do you want me to read it to you?" Emily asked.

Dov shook his head no. If God had a surprise for him, Dov would find out for himself—wherever it took him.

Carefully he opened the letter and read it. And now he was sure of two things: This voyage had just begun.

And he was not alone.

DANGEROUS SPRING

This book is set during the dangerous, unsettled days of spring 1948. The final few weeks leading up to Israel's declaration of independence were very tense. Bad feelings between Arabs and Jews grew daily as the British prepared to leave. The British "Mandate" to govern Palestine would end in May of that year, and for many British, the deadline couldn't come soon enough. Most wanted to go home, and the sooner the better.

Meanwhile, in the years following World War II, thousands of Jews wanted to come to the country of Palestine—and couldn't. They crowded onto any ship they could find—seaworthy or not—in their desperate attempt to reach the Promised Land. Many were intercepted by the British, who were concerned about holding to strict immigration limits. Those who were stopped often ended up in one of the twelve detention camps on Cyprus Island, about two hundred miles northwest of Israel in the Mediterranean Sea. (Cyprus itself is an ancient island settled by Greeks and Turks and is about the size of Massachusetts.)

The first detention camp was opened in August of 1946, while the last detainees left for Israel in February 1949. During the years of its use, fifty-two thousand Jews spent time there, under rules very much like those in prisoner-of-war camps. Over two thousand children were born in the camps. But even with clinics, nurseries, and schools, conditions in the camps were basic and harsh. No, they were a far cry from the Nazi death camps some of the Jews had survived. But the horrible twist of again living behind barbed wire, even after the war was over, made every Jewish prisoner long for freedom and a homeland more than ever.

I'm indebted to several eyewitness accounts of life in the camps, especially *Last Barrier to Freedom* by Morris Laub. Mr. Laub's anecdotes and accounts of his years spent in the camps as an administrator for the American Jewish Joint Distribution Committee gave me a wonderfully detailed framework for my camp scenes—including the Passover, when fresh carp was brought into the camp.

The character of J.D. Roper was inspired by (but not based on) a real-life reporter, I.F. Stone of *PM Magazine*. The real Mr. Stone visited the camps during Passover of 1947 and wrote several interesting accounts of life there from his perspective. These are included in Morris Laub's book, as well.

I also drew much of the camp description from Captain Rudolph Patzert's detailed recollection of his time on Cyprus. What a memory! He writes about coming to the camp as an American—everything from meeting refugee children and getting sick to run-ins with the British. You can find the whole story in a book called *Running the Palestine Brigade* (Naval Institute Press).

What else in our story is real? Certainly the descriptions of Cyprus Island, inspired by the wonderful black-and-white and color photographs of Cyprus native Reno Wideson. Mr. Wideson filled several books with his fine photos—including *Cyprus in Picture* and *Cyprus: Images of a Lifetime.* Looking at one of Mr. Wideson's books is the next best thing to visiting the beautiful island. By the way, the Margoa Jewish Cemetery was and is a real place. However, it's located outside camp boundaries.

Outside of Cyprus, Puah Shteiner's remarkable first-person account of living in the Old City of Jerusalem during 1947 and 1948 also inspired much of this book. What would it be like to live in a walled city, with no way out and under constant attack? The fear and everyday experience of a young girl is captured in *Forever My Jerusalem* (Feldheim Publishers, 1988).

My account of the orphaned girls was inspired by a photo in the April 1996 issue of *National Geographic* magazine showing Franciscan priest Anthony Foley with a group of young orphan boys. As the magazine's caption explains, in 1948 Father Foley singlehandedly led seventy orphans to safety from the Old City war zone to Bethlehem, five miles away. More than anything else, Father Foley's story illustrates doing what Jesus told us to in Matthew 25:40: "Whatever you did for one of the least of these brothers of mine, you did for me." In that verse, Jesus says that when we reach out to the weak and helpless ("these brothers of mine"), it's as if we are serving Him directly—in person. Incredible!

I'm indebted to radio technician Jim Swartos for general information about portable shortwave radio transmitters. Thanks, professor.

And finally, the hanging trolley over the Hinnom Valley really exists, although it wasn't actually built by Jewish forces until late 1948. I couldn't resist using it in this story, however, as a real piece of history. Called Avshalom's Way, this cable linked Jewish positions on Mount Zion with western New City Jerusalem. Although there actually was a tunnel between Yemin Moshe and Mount Zion, it was hard to use. The two-hundred-meter cable car helped Jewish forces evacuate wounded soldiers from the Old City, and because it was lowered every night to help hide it, it was never discovered. In fact, the system was kept in working order up until the 1967 Six-Day War—just in case. Today there's a small museum on the west end of the cable in the basement of what was once the St. John's Ophthalmic Hospital. When my wife, Ronda, and I first saw the cable car there, we knew it had to be a part of one of the PROMISE OF ZION books.

FROM THE AUTHOR

The adventures don't stop with the last page of this book! Here are several ideas for you to try:

1. *Jump into the final adventure, called* True Betrayer.
2. *Discover other books.* I've put together a list of some of my favorite books, magazines, Web sites, music, and more on Israel. They'll help you get a better feel for the strange and wonderful land Dov and Emily came to. Be sure to show this section to your parents or teacher.
3. *Write to me.* I always enjoy hearing from readers, and I answer all my mail. How did you like the book? Did you have a question about anything that happened or about what the characters were thinking? What's next? My address is: Bethany House Publishers, 11400 Hampshire Avenue South, Bloomington, MN, 55438 USA.
4. *Go online.* Visit my Web site at *www.elmerbooks.org.* That's where you can learn more about my books, read a little about me, and find out the answers to many of your questions. Check out *www.bethanyhouse.com,* too, for more of the latest news about PROMISE OF ZION and my other series.

That should keep you busy . . . until the next adventure.

Shalom!

Robert Elmer

WANT TO KNOW MORE?

You're in luck! The library, bookstands, and even the Internet are full of great resources for learning more about Israel and the incredible events that happened there between 1946 and 1949. Here are a few ideas to get you started.

Picture Books on Israel

- *The Bible Lands Holyland Journey* by Dr. Randall D. Smith. Published by Doko in Israel, this is one of the better picture books of Israel and the Holy Land I've found. You'll see pictures of many of the places Dov and Emily visit.

History

- *Front Page Israel* by the *Jerusalem Post* (Jerusalem Post, 1986). This book contains copies of actual newspapers as they appeared between 1932 and 1986. It may be a little hard to locate, but this book is a treasure trove of real-life history.
- *Dawn of the Promised Land* by Ben Wicks (Hyperion, 1997). This book was written for Israel's fiftieth anniversary, and it's very good. It's not exactly a children's book, but there are lots of really interesting interviews with people remembering what it was like to be a kid in the Promised Land in 1948, doing the kinds of things Dov and Emily did.
- *The Best of Zvi* by Zvi Kalisher. This man's story inspired many of the events in Dov Zalinski's life. In fact, I had a chance to interview him personally in his Jerusalem home. What a

story—truth is even more exciting than fiction! The book is available through the Friends of Israel Gospel Ministry in New Jersey, P.O. Box 908, Bellmawr, NJ 08099. They also have an interesting magazine called *Israel, My Glory*.

- *The Creation of Israel* by Linda Jacobs Altman (Lucent Books World History Series, 1998). A good all-in-one history of how Israel was founded, this book has a useful timeline, index, and pictures, too. A perfect resource for a student's research paper.

See also the books I've mentioned in the section titled "Dangerous Spring."

Hebrew

- *Hebrew for Everyone*, published and distributed by Epistle. Here's a fun, kid-friendly approach to learning the language of the Old Testament—and today's Israel! The study guide is written by Jewish believers in Jesus and is designed for kids and beginners. You can learn the Lord's Prayer in Hebrew! I picked up my copy at the Garden Tomb in Jerusalem for twenty shekels. (A shekel is twenty-five cents.) Contact Epistle at P.O. Box 2817, Petach Tikva, 49127, Israel.

Internet

- The International Christian Embassy of Jerusalem (*www.icej.org.il*) is a good place to start for all kinds of links for travel and historical information on Jerusalem and Israel.
- The U.S. Holocaust Memorial Museum (*www.ushmm.org*) is the leading museum in North America for information on what happened to the Jewish people before, during, and after World War II.

Music

- *Hora—The Most Famous 25 Israeli Folk Songs.* Hear some of the songs mentioned in this series, like the song Dov's mom sang, "Yevarechecha." They're fun to listen to, and they'll help you sound out some of those unusual but beautiful Hebrew words!

- *Adonai—The Power of Worship From the Land of Israel* (Integrity Music). Good Messianic music that gives you an excellent flavor of Hebrew-style worship songs. Includes the "Hatikvah," Israel's national anthem.

PREVIEW

The adventures race to an exciting climax in book six of
PROMISE OF ZION, *True Betrayer*.

When Israel declares independence, Dov and Emily are torn
between celebration and frustration. Jerusalem's situation is growing desperate, and Dov escapes in an attempt to reach his mother.
Emily follows him with the help of a secretive stranger, and the
three make their way to Kibbutz Yad Shalom. There, Dov and
Emily enjoy seeing old friends—but can the isolated settlement
survive an attack by Egyptian soldiers and an apparent betrayal?
With danger and conflict all around, how can Dov and his mother
be reunited?